"O... that's a kiss."

Barbara leaned her head back, her eyes rolling to the ceiling, just imagining Chuck kissing her like Damon, the hero of *Mediterranean Magic*.

"I don't believe it." Chuck jerked the book out of her hand and read the steamy passage again.

"Well, don't worry about it." Barbara tried to keep the smugness of her ploy out of her voice. "Nobody said you had to be as good at making love as the guy from this book."

"I'm as good a lover as he is any day!" Chuck insisted.

"If you say so." Barbara let a little disbelief trail into her voice. "Um-m-m—what a man!" she teased.

Suddenly the book was flying across the room as Chuck grabbed her shoulder, his eyes dark with determination. "Come here, woman, and learn what a man *really* is," he growled.

Dixie McKeone, when she isn't writing romances and mysteries, can be found designing subdivisions and streets. Her background includes twelve years in civil engineering and surveying, and she has worked on designs for bridges, superhighways and dams. Her vivid imagination, combined with her unique background and experiences, brings a freshness, an edge of excitement to her writing. She has two grown daughters and lives in La Mesa, California.

Books by Dixie McKeone

HARLEQUIN ROMANCE
2642—CONNOISSEUR'S CHOICE
2722—THE MATCHMAKING DEPARTMENT

HARLEQUIN REGENCY ROMANCE
18—THE WINTER PICNIC

Don't miss any of our special offers. Write to us at the following address for information on our newest releases.

Harlequin Reader Service
901 Fuhrmann Blvd., P.O. Box 1397, Buffalo, NY 14240
Canadian address: P.O. Box 603,
Fort Erie, Ont. L2A 5X3

The Harlequin Hero

Dixie McKeone

Harlequin Books

TORONTO • NEW YORK • LONDON
AMSTERDAM • PARIS • SYDNEY • HAMBURG
STOCKHOLM • ATHENS • TOKYO • MILAN

Original hardcover edition published in 1986
by Mills & Boon Limited

ISBN 0-373-02838-5

Harlequin Romance first edition May 1987
Second printing May 1987

CHAPTER ONE

'But my darling, I've always loved you,' said Damon as his arms drew her closer. 'There was never another woman for me from the moment you walked into my life.'

The moonlight reflected on the water. The gentle waves whispered in rhythm with the song in Melissa's heart. The stars shining in her eyes remained bright as his lips met hers.

The End

WITH a sigh, Barbara Lewis closed the book and tucked it in her handbag. She was still so immersed in the story she could have lived it. The moon, the water, the stardust of the moment still surrounded her. Her cheek tingled with the caress of a strand of hair blown by the soft breeze off the Mediterranean. Sand was in her shoes; her heart and pulse had speeded up with the excitement of the love story and her flesh quivered as she felt those strong arms around her, holding her close.

But there were differences between Barbara's imagery and what the book had created. Instead of the dark unruly curls of the Greek shipping magnate, her fingers ran through soft, light brown waves, sunbleached to blonde on top. The dark eyes that held Melissa spellbound were for Barbara a bright, chameleon hazel that changed shades according to the surroundings or their owner's mood.

They lit with tiny flecks of gold in laughter, they greyed with anger or disappointment. Narrowed with irritation, they glinted slightly green. The depth of colour was a measurement of the intensity behind them. But at that moment they were narrowed, slightly green and darkening. She realised they were two feet in front of her and had been there for some time.

'Damn it, Bab, come out of your dream world! Did East-West call or didn't they?'

The Mediterranean seashore metamorphosed back into a small, shabby little office, brightened by Barbara's efforts. The impeccable white dinner-jacket dissolved into a faded denim shirt with dirt and grease on one shoulder. The well-muscled frame beneath the workshirt was tense as Chuck leaned across the desk. The grey of worry flickered in the greenness of his eyes.

Barbara gazed up at him as she came out of her dream. The other occupant of her pleasant reverie, and incidentally her boss, was repeating his question. Like an echoing memory, she could hear the words he had addressed to her, but the first two times they had failed to penetrate her day dream.

'Uh—yes.' She removed the neatly written order from the stack file. 'Half a load to Santa Barbara, and they want to know if you can pick up a full load in Silicone Valley to bring back.'

'Computers?' Charles Ingram was owner and President of Pacific Trucking. He was also manager, mechanic, and sometimes driver in the small but growing business. He stood the stresses and disappointments and enjoyed each minor victory like a kid with a new toy. With an almost childlike happiness he dropped into a chair across from Barbara's desk. His jeans, fitting like painted fabric, showed off the muscles in his thighs and hips as he turned slightly to take a wrench from his back pocket. He put it on the floor and grinned at Barbara as he leaned back.

'Be great if we could get a toe-hold up there,' he said. His eyes went gold, sparkling with the light of his dream to make Pacific Trucking into a large, profitable business.

Barbara shared that dream, but to her any ambition of Chuck's was worth sharing. She had been in step with his every hope since the first moments of the interview that won her the job eighteen months ago.

To her, Chuck was the epitome of a hero out of a novel, only better, because he was real, there, and when she closed a book, she could think of him as a possibility in her own life, a living breathing hunk.

Unlike the heroes in the books she read, he didn't tower over other men. But five foot ten was perfect for him. He was condensed power. The sparkle of that compactness would have been lost in some hulking brute. His body was well-formed and taut; his muscles could cord and swell with terrific strength when he needed it. The sensuality that hung around him like an aura was too subtle, too unconscious and ingrained to be adequately described. It lingered like a delicate perfume, too light on the air to be noticed, but all the more powerful for its subtlety.

At thirty, his face had yet to take on harsh craggy lines, but determination showed in that squared jaw. His laughter-loving eyes could narrow and glint, his mouth could tighten in a thin line when the occasion demanded, and when he became authoritative, he was head and shoulders above most real and fictional characters. Daily Barbara watched Chuck's will prevail over both men and women, yet lacking any trace of arrogance, it called for neither objection nor resentment.

But none of his heroic attributes were responsible for captivating her heart. She had walked into the office, taken one look and wanted to escape the dust and clutter as soon as possible. As if seeing the room through her eyes, Chuck had jumped to remove a coat from a chair, swept the litter of papers on the desk into a pile on the corner. Then he won her heart as he looked at the rest of the room, his expression indecisive and slightly helpless, as if wondering why, after his efforts, the room was not sparkling and perfect.

She never ceased to be thrilled by his masculinity, but she loved him as much because of his small failures. That little helplessness in the housekeeping of the business provided an opportunity for her to take care of him in a small way. She kept to herself the number of extra hours she put into his comfort.

He was appreciative, she thought, as she watched him turn slightly in the chair. He ran a gentle finger down the edge of a thriving philodendron on the low table by his chair. He was a toucher, silently showing his notice of Barbara's housekeeping efforts. She loved to watch him absently tracing reflections on the dust-free and polished desk and the shining filing-cabinets. His mind might be on a contract or the servicing of a truck, but he would rub away some little spot that threatened to mar the perfection of a shining surface Barbara had just finished cleaning.

'That's a new plant,' he said and hesitated as if some vague memory made him unsure, a walker on the precipice of another's sensitivity.

'I brought it in this morning,' Barbara lied. The plant had been sitting on that table for two weeks. Part of that time he was on a trip to San Francisco because one of his drivers had been ill. And other business pressures, just easing, had freed his mind so he noticed his surroundings again. Yet in her heart the untruth had not been quite a lie. She bought the plant because Chuck enjoyed growing things, and like much of her world, it began its existence with his pleasure.

He looked down at his watch and whistled. 'The five-o'clock whistle blew over an hour ago. Why are you still here?'

Barbara took care to look surprised. 'I had no idea it was so late,' she replied. She knew the time, but it too was relative to Chuck. The day didn't end until they shared it. He had been outside all afternoon, giving his new acquisition, a second-hand tractor-trailer, a thorough maintenance check. His policy of doing for himself what he could was a plus for the business, but often it was a distinct disadvantage to Barbara's romantic plans.

'Well, I'm tired of the place for the day,' he grumbled. 'How about some face-filling?'

Oh, how romantic, Barbara thought. 'Great,' was what she said.

'Take me a bit to get the grease off',' he said, getting up from the chair. In a moment he was off down the short hall. The tiny converted house that served as a company office still had a fully equipped bathroom with a shower. Chuck had added a cupboard. Being able to make a fast switch from greasy mechanic to polished executive within a few minutes had its advantages.

Barbara straightened her desk, put the cover on her typewriter and reached for her handbag. She had to remove the just-finished novel as she reached for her comb and cosmetic case. She was combing her hair when her eyes strayed from her reflection to the front cover of the book. She noticed the similarity between the picture on the front of the cover and what she saw in the mirror.

The hair colour was almost identical. Blonde, light enough to attract attention, both she and the heroine had a certain unevenness of shading that only appeared in natural blondes. Melissa's hung free; Barbara kept hers back in a luxuriant bun at the nape of her neck.

Melissa of the book could boast no bluer eyes, but she had an edge on beauty. Barbara was under no delusion that she was superstar material, but her face was adequate, she thought. Her nose was a little too pert, but—she picked up the book and brought the picture closer —Melissa had a small nose too.

Barbara put the book down and pursed her lips as she looked at the overall effect. Melissa looked a little haughty on the cover. Barbara knew she could never be the haughty type, she was more likely to grin like an idiot, but men liked pleasant expressions.

Why couldn't I be on the cover of a book? she wondered. *Better still, why can't I be the heroine and never mind the cover?*

She put the make-up back in her handbag and sat looking at the book, thinking about the story. There were similarities in the two situations, she thought. Melissa's Damon was the enormously wealthy owner of a huge shipping line. Chuck owned a shipping firm too. He wasn't wealthy, and most of the money he earned went back into the company and his five diesel trucks, but after all, shipping was shipping.

'And I have an advantage—I know he's fond of me,' Barbara told the female on the cover. 'He just needs a little push to fall in love.' She couldn't be too wrong about that, she thought. When she started her job a year and a half before, she was sure he would never notice her. A sultry-voiced female had been calling Chuck regularly, but gradually over a period of several months, the sultriness changed to impatience and then to imperious demands.

Sandy's insistence grew along with his urgent business pressures. Over the months his face had changed, his easy-going smile had been lost under the tautness of a tension that never seemed to leave him. Barbara had mourned for that helpless look in his eyes. He was torn in the battle of his two loves—the woman in his life and his company that had to be nurtured into healthy growth.

At first Barbara was delighted when Sandy stopped calling, but her happiness couldn't last in the face of Chuck's pain. Life seemed to die out of his eyes. She could feel the chill of the grey fog that surrounded him. All the fun, all the enjoyment of his growing business faded with his hurt. Then, over the months, he had turned to her for company. They often went out for a bite to eat, and he started calling at her flat in the evenings to chat.

As if coming out of a long and debilitating illness, his spirits had revived.

Their relationship would have been wonderful if there had been anything lover-like in his attentions. His conversation was all business, but they were together so often now that his limited time away from her prevented the possibility of another woman in his life. A week before they had stopped in a local spot to hear a new band, and he had seemed jealous of an attractive stranger who asked Barbara to dance.

'So you see, I've got an edge,' Barbara said to the front cover of the book. And love is like anything else, it has to be fed or it starves.' Was the picture on the front of the book really haughty, or just knowledgeable?

Pleased with her assessment of the situation, Barbara tucked the book in her handbag and sat back, waiting for Chuck to reappear. She smiled at her own nonsense in talking to the girl on the cover, and let her mind slide into the plans for next Monday's work. She was wondering about the need for a new filing-cabinet when the phone rang.

The cold draft from the grave of all her hopes washed

over Barbara when she heard the one voice she dreaded.

'Is Mr Ingram available at the moment?' The caller was Sultry Sandy. She spoke with the preciseness of a condescending adult to a half-witted child.

Barbara was a moment trying to find her voice, to bring her thoughts in order. For a moment she thought wildly of saying Chuck had sold the business and was now a beachcomber on some desert island in the Pacific, but she knew that wouldn't do. She raised her head, listening. She could no longer hear the shower running, but his absent whistling, reaching her through closed doors, meant he was still dressing.

'No, he's not available at the moment—can he return your call?' Barbara responded in her best secretary voice. She hoped it was adequate.

'I'll be out for the evening, but I'll call again tomorrow. I trust I can reach him then?' Sandy's inflection intimated she thought Barbara was at fault, but one allowed certain failings in underlings, provided they did not inconvenience one too much. Without waiting for an answer, Sandy hung up.

Barbara replaced the receiver on the hook and stared at the phone.

'You—you—*Zelda*,' she hurled the words, hoping they would reach the woman at the other end of the line, and wishing Sandy knew what an insult it was. Zelda had been the 'other woman' in the book she had read, and the similarity had struck Barbara the moment she heard Sandy's voice on the phone.

Another similarity, Barbara realised as she thought over the story line. Zelda had been trying to coerce the fictional hero, Damon, into marrying her by political pressure. From overheard telephone conversations, Barbara was reasonably sure Sandy was trying to lure Chuck with her father's money. Barbara wasn't worried about that. Chuck was neither money nor power-hungry. He was achievement-oriented, taking more pleasure in his own successful efforts than the financial reward they brought.

And Sandy wanted to make him into something he wasn't, trying to get him into the country-club set. That had caused another argument the door of his office hadn't kept secret. When he learned Sandy's parents had put him up for membership without his permission, he had shouted at his lady-love. But apparently she had not given up trying to smooth his rough edges and give him social polish.

The last idea she surmised from the only remark he ever made about their relationship.

'She discovered silk purses really can't be made of sows' ears,' he had said with a dreadful finality.

Barbara had not answered; how did she tell him Sandy, looking from the heights of her pseudo-values, was the epitome of stupidity?

'I hope you haven't discovered what a fool you are,' Barbara muttered to the phone, doubting all the time her hope was justified.

At that moment Chuck came striding into the room. A sheen of fresh scrubbing was on his skin; he had changed into a pair of jeans and polished cowboy boots, and wore a cream and blue western-style shirt tailored to fit his wide chest and tapering waist. He never fussed over his hair, so it was wet and combed neatly, but the drying ends were waving to suit themselves.

As Barbara opened her mouth to speak, he raised his hand, stopping her.

'I heard the phone—I don't want to know who it was. Let's go bite something. Clients can wait till tomorrow.' His mood was happy, freer than it had been for weeks. Barbara loved it when his eyes danced.

'But—' She tried to override him, thinking he should know about Sandy, no matter what her personal feelings were.

His brows snapped down. 'Has Frank, Sam, or Otis been in an accident?' He was the type to worry about his long-distance drivers.

'No, but—'

'Then don't tell me,' he repeated, digging in his pocket for his keys. 'I'm hungry, I'm tired, and the office is closed. Come on, woman, or I'll lock you in.'

'I tried,' Barbara said as she picked up her handbag and hurried for the door. 'You remember that—I tried.'

In her battered Volkswagen, Barbara followed Chuck as automatically as if she were being towed. By the direction he took, she could tell his plans for the evening. He was heading for her flat. By the custom of months, they would not go in. They would park either her car or his, and head for one of their favourite restaurants. Later they would return to sit in front of her television or just talk.

Tonight she was particularly grateful for that. If he refused to let her tell him about the call, she still had one night of his company before Sandy intruded into his life again.

Born with an optimistic mind, she fought the depression that threatened to settle over her. Perhaps Sandy had left her compact in his jeep, and that was the only reason for her call, she thought.

Don't be dumb, she warned herself. *Sandy wouldn't be caught dead riding in that jeep, they always took her sports-car.*

Still following Chuck, Barbara thrust her chin forward, glowering at the traffic-lights that had caught both her and Chuck. Sandy wasn't just walking in and taking over without a battle, she decided.

'She doesn't really love him,' Barbara stared at the street ahead. 'She doesn't know what it takes to make him happy. I'll fight her every inch of the way.' The idea sounded great, but she frowned over how to put it into practice.

As the woman in the next car smiled and quickly averted her face, Barbara realised she had been speaking aloud, and the car windows were down. As she followed the jeep across the intersection, her face could have stopped traffic with its embarrassed glow.

Her worries over Sandy were momentarily submerged under a more immediate concern. The car was sputtering. Her eyes flew to the fuel gauge. Not the problem. And it certainly shouldn't be. She had filled the tank the day before.

She would ask Chuck to take a look at it. He took care of her car as well as the trucks and his jeep—a convenient and undeclared bonus of the job, as she often thought of it.

They made the circuit of their usual haunts, growing hungrier and more impatient at every stop. They had returned to the bar and grill around the corner from the office where they often dashed in for a quick sandwich during the day. By the resignation in his voice when he ordered, Chuck had wanted something more than a hot pastrami on rye and a beer.

'Well finally,' Chuck growled at Barbara after the waitress slapped the plates on the table and walked away. Barbara didn't blame him. He had worked hard all day and she knew he was hungry. A Friday evening was no time to be late leaving the office. Most of their favourite restaurants were filled and had queues of customers waiting.

'We should have stayed at my place—I *can* cook,' Barbara said as Chuck eyed the sandwich with distaste.

She knew the response that would bring from him, a quick, impatient shake of the head, causing his lively sandy waves to bounce. She had always liked his theory that the working woman should stand over the kitchen stove at night only if she really wanted to cook. His thoughtfulness would be a blessing to his wife when he married.

'You're paying anyway,' he replied, looking irritated as he vainly patted his jeans, shirt and jacket.

Barbara smiled tenderly at him as he continued to check his back pockets. He acted as if his missing wallet might be hiding from him. That was one of his little foibles that always amused her. She had long since learned to bring enough money to cover their needs in an emergency, knowing it would be returned to her at the next opportunity. She opened her handbag, pulling out her own wallet. As she did so the book, *Mediterranean Magic*, fell to the floor.

'What's this?' Chuck picked up the book and turned it over, looking at the cover. The picture of the two handsome people on the front cover gave an instant impression of love and innocence.

'A book,' Barbara answered with the obvious.

'I don't have time for reading any more,' Chuck said. He turned the romantic novel over, and read aloud the blurb on the back cover:

'I didn't ask you to come into my life, Melissa, but you came, and now you stay. You are my woman. Don't ever forget it.'

Chuck looked up, grinning. 'If I said that to a chick, I'd probably be picking up my teeth.'

Barbara opened her mouth to object, but he continued reading:

Damon was staring into her eyes, mesmerising Melissa with his hypnotic gaze, but his dark lashes flickered as he noticed her empty glass. As always, he was considerate of her every wish.

'Waiter,' he commanded, snapping his fingers imperiously, 'the lady would like more champagne.'

Chuck laughed and handed her the book. 'Fairy tales,' he remarked.

Barbara, irked that a story she had enjoyed was being maligned, took it with ill-concealed impatience.

'Think anything you want, but personally I prefer that to sitting here like this.' She picked up the empty beer glass and held it for emphasis. 'At least the guy in the book was considerate.'

Chuck frowned and turned his head towards the bar across the room.

'Hey, Sarah!' he shouted.. 'Two more beers and easy on the heads!'

Barbara put the glass down with a thump of finality. 'You're right,' she said glumly. 'Damon could say anything to a woman and get the right response. *You* would be picking up your teeth.'

Chuck look puzzled as he stopped eating his sandwich, holding it in mid-air.

'What did I do?'

Barbara looked at him and sighed, shaking her head. 'You ordered a beer. Thank you.'

Later, Barbara and Chuck went back to her flat. As usual, by Friday evening, the work and worries of the week had been fatiguing, and they liked to spend those evenings resting. Through the months they had developed a habit of relaxing, lazily rehashing events and generally unwinding.

Chuck leaned against the counter, while Barbara fed the necessities to the automatic-drip coffee-pot. When she turned it on, she followed him into her small living-room.

'. . . So who knows, maybe we'll get another driver if we can get contracts up in Silicone Valley,' Chuck was saying. He sat at the end of the couch, his feet propped on the coffee-table, the polished walnut surface protected by a small sofa cushion Barbara left there just for him.

'I sure am glad East-West came through with that order,' Barbara replied, curling up in her favourite rocking chair. She liked to sit where she could observe him. Relaxed and in a good mood, he filled the room with a special nuance of pleasure when he was there.

Chuck smiled slowly and clasped his hands behind his neck, looking up at the ceiling. 'Yea, we're getting ready to move. Now if Samuels comes through too—' He lowered his arms and sat up, his eyes bright. 'That wasn't Samuels on the phone this afternoon, was it?'

Cold washed over Barbara. For a while she had forgotten that call. She shook her head, hoping he would not ask.

'Okay, what was it? The way you're keeping it secret—'

'I did not,' Barbara snapped. 'I tried to tell you and you wouldn't let me.' She couldn't let him think she deliberately didn't tell him. 'Then I forgot it.'

'Well who was it—am I being dunned—sued—?' He rubbed his hands together and grinned in mock anticipation. 'Did some hot chick leave me an obscene message?'

'I don't know if she was a hot chick, and she wasn't obscene,' Barbara replied. 'It was Sandy.'

Chuck didn't answer. Slowly his face changed. His eyes looked into the distance, the eyes of a Christmas child, holding the wonder of a dream made reality. The happiness of a hopeless cause suddenly coming to fruition glowed from him and scorched Barbara until she wanted to cry out.

After his break-up with Sandy, she had recognised his pain, worried over his loss of spirit, but she had taken his mood to be one of wounded ego. She had not realised or had not allowed herself to believe he could have been in love with the socialite.

She wanted to scream at him, to tell him how stupid he was to want a woman who was so unfeeling and selfish as to walk out on him a year ago. But if she was any smarter, would she be in love with a man who loved another woman?

'What did she say?' His voice was hoarse, though he made an effort to control it.

'She said she'd call back tomorrow. I didn't get a chance to remind her the office will be closed.' Barbara forced out the words, wishing she could say Sandy was leaving tonight for Timbuctoo, wishing she could lie and backstab and do terrible things. But without the experience, she didn't know how, and even if she had, to hurt Chuck was the last thing she wanted.

Feeling as if her feet weighed a ton, she went to the kitchen and fixed a tray with the coffee. Back in the living-room she put it on the low table, poured for herself and Chuck, and resumed her place.

Absently he thanked her for the coffee, drinking it black. He never drank it black.

Barbara was hurt by his absentmindedness. She tried to bring his mind back into the room with her.

'Maybe Samuels will call on Monday,' she said.

'Uh-huh,' he answered. No enthusiasm.

'Would be nice,' Barbara went on. 'Then all we have to do is pick up the two trucks that have turned over—' She waited for a reaction and received none. 'I tried to pick them up by myself, you know,' she went on. 'But after running thirty-five miles up the freeway on a broken leg, I was out of breath.'

'Yeah.' Chuck's attentiveness and response left something to be desired.

Barbara too stared out into the distance. Two words had destroyed her world. All she had to say was 'Sandy called,' and she ceased to exist in Chuck's mind.

Well, if she didn't count, she wasn't going to make him more coffee and watch him dream about another woman.

'Why don't you go home?' she snapped.

'Yeah, it's been a rough week, you're tired, I guess.' His mind was elsewhere. Her flare of temper went unnoticed.

The arm he dropped across her shoulders as she walked him to the door was the affection of a friend. Somehow that too hurt, when only the week before she was thrilled by it.

Barbara closed the door behind him and automatically moved about, washing up the coffee things and putting them away. Enfolded in a blanket of emptiness, she was for a while beyond thinking.

Then the whips of memory struck at her. Chuck standing by the filing-cabinet, one careful finger tracing the reflection on a polished surface; his firm decisiveness when executive matters were at stake, and that little helplessness when he couldn't find a telephone number.

The cuts in Sandy's voice had proved her to be a selfish, conceited woman. She had seen in Chuck only the gorgeous creature that appeared on the surface. Sandy wanted a man who would turn her friends green with jealousy when she walked into a room on his arm. She'd never notice those little things that took nothing from his masculinity, yet made him so endearing.

Would Sandy have plants around because he liked

living things? He was too busy and too erratic in his time in the office to look after them, but Barbara knew his eyes often strayed to the thriving pots of philodendron. She'd seen him brush a speck of dust from a shining leaf, and if she didn't hide the watering can he made up for his inattention by drowning them.

Barbara shook her head, answering her own questions. Sandy had other things in mind. She wanted the life she was used to. Chuck would be worked to death, trying to increase his business, wanting to give her everything she wanted. He would run himself to death trying to make a life she desired, and before long he would be a burned-out shell.

Barbara had seen it happen. Back in her home town in Iowa, a member of her mother's bridge club was a grasping selfish woman. Her husband was a man who no longer enjoyed life; he endured it.

She shut off the water at the kitchen sink with a force that could have wrenched out the handle. That was not going to happen to Chuck! He might be stupid when it came to women, but he was a nice stupid; a generous, giving stupid whose life shouldn't be ruined by a grasping female.

She turned off the light in the kitchen and headed for the bedroom. How did one fight a woman like Sandy? She was designing, so Barbara would be designing too. Maybe she should be a little selfish too, just enough to give herself more value in his mind. Yes, it could work. After all, since she was in the office, she spent more time with him than Sandy, and that should work to her advantage.

In the bedroom she flipped on the light and came face to face with her reflection in the mirror across the room. She was no competition for a socialite in the clothes she wore to the office. Jeans were practical when she might have to climb into a trailer to find Chuck for a telephone call, but she had been getting sloppy. Then and there she made a rule. No more jeans, no matter what she climbed.

A flick of her mind brought her the latest figures of her bank balance. She was proud of the way it was growing. Her sudden decision would deplete it.

When she retired, she might have to live in a dress box, but she would spend the next day shopping.

And she thought there must be other things she could do. She remembered her silly thoughts that afternoon about being a heroine from a book. The idea was taking on a sudden seriousness. Maybe, just maybe, the answer to her problem lay in those pages.

'Melissa—where are you?' she called out as if the book could answer. She turned towards the living-room to find her handbag where *Mediterranean Magic* rested in the side pocket.

CHAPTER TWO

BARBARA kept her promise to herself, and by the next afternoon her bank account was severely depleted, and her feet were aching but her new image had been accomplished. Her weekend was lonely, and the new clothes could not alleviate the pain of the silent phone, the door that echoed no knock.

She wrote a duty letter to her mother and father. As usual, she included two paragraphs on the weather, one of her father's primary interests, since he was a farmer. That helped fill the space and allowed her, also as usual, to skip answering her mother's questions about the men in her life. Her mother would be uneasy until Barbara had a wedding-ring on her finger. Now that Sandy had re-entered the picture, that time might be far away.

She arrived early for work on Monday morning. As she parked the Volkswagen, she made a mental note to tell Chuck about the misbehaviour of the car. Saturday it had behaved perfectly, but that morning it was kicking up again. Usually the trucks were on the road before she opened the office, but believing her new image would take some time to perfect, she had been up and moving about at dawn.

Otis and Frank were ready to roll when she stepped out of the battered Volkswagen. Their whistles told her that her day of shopping and her depleted bank account had not been spent in vain.

Her new hair-do, facial, manicure and wardrobe were at least a start on her plan to make herself some competition for the other woman in Chuck's life.

23

The convenient bun was gone. In its place her blonde hair hung in a chic straight-cut pageboy that came just to her collar. After a lengthy discussion between three hairdressers, the style they had chosen for her had been exactly the same as the one shown on the cover of *Mediterranean Magic*. When Barbara had returned home and compared herself to the cover of the book, she had felt a thrill that was illogical but no less real. The similarity in looks had made her feel as if her far-fetched plan would succeed. It seemed as if the power of love had given her a 'go,' and she could move forward with complete confidence.

The price of the little blue linen 'frock' with its white piping had caused her checkbook to wilt at the edges, but it shouted allure with a subtlety that made it a trap worth having. The delicately-strapped high-heeled sandals were perfect with it.

And the result was making a profound impression on its intended victim, but apparently not the kind Barbara had hoped for. Chuck had been standing in the open doorway of the office, watching as Otis and Frank pulled out. Now he eyed her coming across the paved lot as if he didn't recognise her. Then his brows lowered as if he thought something was wrong. His expression could not have been more ludicrous if she had arrived at work in her bathrobe.

A momentary panic hit Barbara as she wondered if she had been wrong in her choice of imagery, but she discarded the idea. After all, it would take some getting used to. Even she had done a double take at the mirror this morning while she was making the bed.

She raised her chin, adding her new poise to the picture and continued for a few steps before coming to an abrupt halt. Her left heel caught in a crack in the asphalt paving. Her mouth fell open with surprise and she jiggled her foot, trying to work it loose. Apparently there was more to this *femme fatale* bit than she at first imagined.

Chuck had disappeared back into the office, coming out again immediately with a clipboard. As he stepped through the door the telephone started to ring.

'Barbara, will you get that?' he shouted without looking in her direction. He continued across the lot, passing her at an angle, intently reading from the papers on the board.

Barbara wiggled her foot, but she was stuck tight. She looked down, wondering if she should take her shoe off and run for the phone. As expensive as those little wispy sandals were, she certainly wasn't jerking her foot and ruining them. But she decided against removing her foot and racing for the phone in her nylons. Her stockings were also new, and too costly to destroy for a phone call.

The phone-ringing continued. In between its bursts of noise, she heard Chuck's footsteps, hurrying, slowing, then stopping altogether.

'Barbara?' he shouted.

She didn't answer. Part of her new attire could not be purchased in any shop. The poise and aplomb she had donned with great deliberation and no little practice. She was not lightly discarding it. Screaming was not a part of her new found dignity, and frustration made any sensible tone of voice impossible. She kept trying to work her foot loose without success.

I will not panic, I will not lose my temper, she told herself. *I am above all this.* But one look down at the shoe said she was only an inch above it. Every time she moved her foot, the heel worked in deeper.

By the time the phone stopped ringing, she heard Chuck's footsteps again, this time hurrying towards her. She tried to keep herself from looking around, but she couldn't resist it. Relief flowed over her as she saw him coming with a crowbar. He knelt and prized at the alligatored section of asphalt that held her trapped. In a moment her foot was free. She looked fearfully at her new footwear, but it was undamaged, apart from some black streaks she thought were removable.

'If you're going to wear those crazy things, you'd better park on the street,' he told her shortly.

Barbara wanted to retort in kind. 'Crazy things' was not the description she had in mind when she bought them.

Wisps of whimsy, for fairy feet, had been what Damon had called Melissa's shoes. So—Chuck was not the type to make flowery speeches—he could have been a little complimentary. But she held her feelings in check. She was determined to use every trick possible to beat out Sandy from his affection, and fighting with him was not a part of her plan.

'Thank you. I don't know what I would have done without you,' she murmured

If his masculine pride had been inflated by her remark he hid it well. He did take her arm, but his grasp was perfunctory as he pulled her away from the cracked spots in the paving.

'Don't get stuck again. I've got too much to do to be digging you out all day—I'd never noticed how bad this surface is. I'd better have it repaired.'

Great! She'd changed her image and all that brought to his mind was repairing the paving. She bit her tongue and reminded herself that bitchiness tended to cancel out assets, no matter how great they were. The fabric of her poise and aplomb was going to need some reinforcement.

'You always know what has to be done,' Barbara said, continuing with her flattery. Why, she wondered, did

similar remarks sound so good in front of her mirror and
so phony in front of Chuck?

And he too had caught the sudden difference in her
attitude. He followed her into the office. As she took her
seat behind her desk, he stood over her frowning.

'What's all this new stuff?' He waved his hand, in-
dicating her hair-do and clothing. 'And what's with the
miss-priss talking? Don't do it on the phone. If Samuels
calls, they'll think they have the wrong number.'

'I don't know what you mean,' Barbara said stiffly,
trying to hide the hurt she felt. Had everything she did,
everything she spent been for nothing? If he didn't like
the new Barbara, all her efforts and money was wasted.
She turned in her chair and with shaking hands put the
costly new handbag on top of the filing-cabinet. As she
turned back she saw his eyes on the handbag. With a
quick movement he stepped around the desk and with a
jerk he pulled the copy of *Mediterranean Magic* from
the outside pocket.

She cringed as his eyes travelled from the cover to her
and back again. With a look of disgust, he threw the
book on the desk.

'You've read too much of this junk! Now you want to
look and act like some character out of a book. The next
time I turn around you'll be running off to—to—' he
picked up the book again, turning it over to scan the
back cover before he threw it down again. 'To Greece or
some such place.'

Her emotions took a dive as he had so quickly divined
part of her reasoning. Not being able to tell him the
truth, letting him continue to think she was foolish
enough to live in a daydream was too much. Disappointment, then frustration coming on top of it was more than
she could stand.

'I hadn't believed you could be so dense and so

wrong,' she lashed out at him. 'The hairstyle is a coincidence. I just decided it was time for a new image.'

'What was wrong with the old image?' Chuck demanded.

'If it was so great, then my door stands up too well against my love-struck suitors,' Barbara retorted. She wondered if she should have said that. Maybe it was a good idea—if it gave him romantic notions.

'Well, I liked the old you,' he growled, looking less sure of his indignation.

But you didn't love the old me, Barbara thought. *You fell in love with Sandy, with the chic and svelte, and liked me because I was comfortable.*

'It was time for a change,' she said.

'I think it was a damn silly thing to do. It's phony. It's not you.'

That was the straw-weight of disapproval that bore her down. She stared up at Chuck, totally angry at him for the first time in their acquaintance. Her new dignity dissolved. Now it was shout or cry. She chose shouting.

'You have no idea what *is* me!' she stormed at him. 'Maybe I want other things out of life! Sneakers and jeans are fine if you plan on staying at a truck stop forever, but some people demand more—they won't settle for that!'

She bit her traitorous tongue but it was too late. She would have done anything to take back those words, but they were said. She was lashing out her hurt, but in doing so she had inadvertently described Sandy's attitude. Would he think she was as selfish as the socialite?

Chuck had paled. He looked as if he had been slapped by one of his own diesel trucks. For a long, silent moment they were still, their gazes locked. Then he slowly crossed the room, moving as if the wind had been knocked out of him. He went into his office and closed the door.

Barbara felt the sting of tears, but she refused to give way. If she did, her emotions would overwhelm her completely. Instead she tried to shut off her mind. She busied herself with small chores that could be done in a stupor. She dusted her desk with a tissue. She sharpened her pencils. She sorted the mail into two piles, business and advertising.

Then she saw the envelope. Chuck had a habit of dropping his outgoing mail in any pile that was handy. She picked it up, wondering if it deserved a trip to the letter-box for the early collection, or if it would wait with the rest until evening. She read the address, hoping it would give her a clue, and what she saw seemed to be the death-knell to her hopes. It was addressed to the country club, and by holding it to the light, she could see the cheque inside.

All her little morning chores were complete and the coffee was busily dripping when Chuck came out of his office. Without looking in her direction he walked across the room and took the chair by the philodendron.

With a savagery she had never seen in him, he snapped a leaf off the plant and slapped it against his open palm.

'So you think this get-up is going to make a difference in your life.' His voice was flat, accusing.

She wanted to cry out, to say, 'Please, isn't it enough I tried and failed, do you have to rub it in?' But her pride would never allow that. And she had suffered enough from his disapproval. She wasn't taking his insults.

'I suppose so, since I believe it will make a difference in me.' She was clipped, short, and sounded like her third-year teacher. 'Man gets what he resembles, not what he deserves.' That was not quite the quote as she had read it, but the meaning was the same. 'I suppose that goes for women too.'

Again their gazes met. His was hard, the hazel eyes almost colourless as he stared at her. Why, she wondered, had she suddenly become his enemy? Over a haircut and a change of costume? His attitude made no sense at all. After a long moment he looked away. His belligerence eased, then returned.

'But you *expect* something out of it, or you wouldn't be trying!' He stood up and strode over to the coffee-brewer, removing the pot and pouring a cup, letting the still-dripping coffee run on to the hotplate beneath. Barbara watched, amazed. He was not fastidious, but he never deliberately made a mess and left it for her to clean. In his agitation he seemed not to notice the spilling coffee or the hiss and bubble when he replaced the glass pot.

As he walked back by her desk he stopped, pointing the philodendron leaf at her as if making a judgment.

'You *do* expect something!' he demanded.

'I don't expect to work here—' Barbara checked herself just in time. In her anger, she had almost given notice before she caught herself. No sensible person left over a difference in opinion on life styles, a little spilled coffee and a torn leaf, particularly when she had just spent most of her savings. She rattled a bit, trying to cover what she had started to say. 'I don't expect to work here for ever.' That required something to accompany it. 'One of these days I'm going to fall in love, and someone will fall in love with me, and I'll be gone. When that time comes I want to be the best I can be—he will deserve that,' she finished breathlessly. She couldn't believe she'd almost resigned. She couldn't believe she'd rattled on about being in love, either, but anything was better than walking out, and she'd almost made that necessary. Her impetuosity had sobered her; she wasn't that mad at Chuck.

She had been so caught up in her own problems she had not at first noticed his expression. She was surprised at him for the second time. He had apparently run into that truck again. He turned back towards his office, but this time he stood with one hand on the door, looking back at her.

'Well, *I'm* not going to do it!' he yelled. 'I'm *me*, and I'm not changing into something else!' He slammed the door.

Barbara stared at the closed door, wondering what happened. '*He's* not changing?' She tried to go over the conversation in her mind, but it didn't make any sense. She tried it again, this time aloud. 'So I said . . . but apparently he didn't accept that, because he said . . .' She thought it over again and tried repeating what he had said. 'He's *not* changing? He's not *changing*?' Moving the emphasis didn't help. One of them definitely had a screw loose.

The phone rang. Barbara answered it and spent ten minutes talking to an insurance adjustor about a damaged shipment. After a full dose of life, business was a relief. But business was slow starting that Monday morning and life was boiling over. She had hardly hung up the phone when Chuck came out of the office again, taking the chair. This time he spared the plant. Barbara watched him warily, but he was quiet, deep in thought. But when he spoke he snarled.

'People ought to be what they are.'

Barbara closed her eyes. She could only take so much emotional battering. Much more of the argument and broke or not, she was going to take her new handbag and walk out.

'If people get phony, nothing works,' Chuck said.

'Look, you lay off!' Barbara snapped back. 'I have had it!' The tears were stinging her eyes again. 'It's not phony to be all you can be. I haven't lost anything but a handful of hair. I've even got my old tennis shoes.'

'That's a profound observation on life, I suppose?'

'Maybe,' Barbara replied hesitantly. She wasn't absolutely sure. 'I've still got the jeans, the sneakers—I can still wear them if I choose. They're just moved over in the cupboard. There was space in the cupboard and space in me, I think.' She raised her chin to give herself courage. 'I'm no longer limiting myself. I'm out to be all I can be.' Did she have to sound so melodramatic? If he laughed out loud, she couldn't blame him.

But he didn't laugh. He was quiet for a moment, thoughtful. When he looked up the anger had dissipated. 'You're saying you're not changing—you're adding something. Like taking a course? Say, if you went to school and learned to speak German, it's a new dimension—the rest of you is just the same?'

'I guess so,' she answered warily, wondering what had come over him, wondering where this new conversation was leading.

He stood up and walked over to the desk, picking up the copy of *Mediterranean Magic*. Barbara tensed. She wished she had never seen that book. Seated again he opened it, read a moment and then looked up.

'I can't believe any woman in her right mind would expect a man to act like that. It's stupid. Unreasonable.'

Barbara wondered how she could be considered unreasonable because of the author's description of the hero. But the time for denials was over. If he was going to insult her, she could fight back. With her fists clenched in her lap, she lashed out at Chuck.

'Oh, is it? That remark is just a part of the male double standard. Every man wants a woman to be his dream girl, but we're supposed to settle for slobs and be grateful, I suppose? A man thinks his woman should be beautiful, intelligent, a perfect hostess, but she's to put up with dirty socks and beer cans in the living-room! Well, if that dreamboat wants to walk in here and sweep me off my feet, I'll have the broom ready for him. Any woman would!'

During her tirade Chuck had been still. When she finished, he leaned forward, the book caught between his clasped hands. His eyes were burning with intensity.

'Any woman?' he asked slowly.

'Almost any woman—unless she was interested in someone else. But I think—' Suddenly Barbara *did* think. He wasn't condemning her, he was fighting the idea because while he disliked it, he saw it as a possible answer to his problems with Sandy.

She sat hardly breathing, knowing she had stumbled on to the truth, but trying to deny it. The whole concept was impossible. Chuck was his own man; he could never be a carbon copy of someone else. But if he loved Sandy enough? Barbara held her breath. With relief she watched the change in his expression. His independent, obstinate nature was asserting itself again.

'Not many men could live up to that,' he said, his voice almost petulant, his eyes harried. He pulled at the neat band of his t-shirt that made a white 'v' at the opening of his denim collar as if he too needed to breathe. 'I'm too busy for that stuff. I'm a good truck driver. I'm a damn good mechanic. My business is getting off the ground with no help from anybody. Why isn't that enough for a woman?'

Barbara wanted to tell him it was—for any sensible woman, but she knew logic would never penetrate his suffering, questioning mind. She hurt for him in his dilemma, and for herself, because she wasn't the one in his heart. She wanted to scream at him to turn to her, and he'd never have to worry about not having his woman's approval, but he needed the unemotional truth. She looked him straight in the eye.

'For some women that *is* enough. For some it's not. It's up to you to make the choice.' But he had made his choice, and it wasn't her.

'I'm not going to be a pantywaist for anybody,' he muttered.

'Well, don't fight me about it.' Barbara busied herself sharpening the already sharp pencils, hoping he would hold to that attitude. She was sorry she ever had the idea to spruce herself up. Her defence had nearly convinced him. If he rejected the concept, Sandy would tire of him as quickly as before. That lady wanted a man who knew his way around more than an eighteen-wheeler.

'But then, it's just a matter of learning some things,' Chuck muttered, more to himself than to Barbara. 'Might be good to know you could go anywhere and not make a fool of yourself.'

Barbara listened, wishing he would get around to his objections again. Suppose he did turn himself into the personification of a story-book hero? With determination, he could do it, and Sandy would be delighted. Barbara would be an also-ran, and Chuck would never know she was in the race.

She was mentally scurrying around, trying to find some way of discouraging him when the door opened. Mrs Washington, the accountant, came in, scattering papers, and looking as if she had been delivered by tornado.

Chuck jumped to grab a folder that skittered across the floor and liberally deposited tax forms on its way.

Rushing around the desk, Barbara grabbed the battered attaché case that was too full to close. They rushed

Mrs Washington into the back office before the rest of her records spilled all over the floor. Chuck brought the little grey-haired woman a cup of coffee.

Barbara shook her head over the instant litter that sprang up around the disorganised but brilliant accountant, and gathered up the records for her inspection.

While she was engaged with Mrs Washington, Chuck stuck his head in the door of the back office. Barbara only half heard his remark about running some errands.

Probably joining Sandy for lunch, Barbara thought as she tried to decipher a weird scribble in the asset column of her books. Most of the work she could handle, but as a bookkeeper she was a complete failure.

Back in her office she looked over some bills of lading, making sure they were all signed. She typed invoices, cleaned up the burned-on coffee from the hotplate and thought about Chuck. She kept telling herself not to worry, he would never turn into the social butterfly Sandy wanted. He was too much of a man to let a woman change him.

He was too much of a man. The thought kept turning itself over in her mind, and some of the connotations were not reassuring. Chuck was a considerate, generous person. His feelings about allowing her to cook for him after work was a prime example. He refused selfishly to take. He gave. When he settled on the woman in his life he would be a giver, a giver of the small things, like compliments that helped her get through a rough day. Barbara had known those little remarks, given so offhand they nearly skipped the mind, but settled in the heart.

Barbara thought of those strong, capable hands that kept the trucks in top mechanical shape and casually managed those eighteen-wheelers on the road. They were gentle hands, touching, appreciative, and they could busy themselves in her kitchen when she suffered a rough day. He would make the coffee or bring out a cold beer for her.

No, she thought, feeling defeated, he would not throw Sandy's wishes away lightly. Gifts that could be purchased, she would have, but he wouldn't stop there. He would give her the gift of recognising what she valued, and try to live up to it. That was what he had been saying.

Adding to yourself—was that the way he had put it? She couldn't remember, but the meaning was the same. She could see his reasoning, the way he said it. He made an effort to study subjects that affected his business. Once he fought it through in his mind, he would feel he owed a loved one as much.

'Damn you, Chuck,' Barbara muttered. 'There are good guys, and good guys, but you're going to carry this too far!'

She knew him too well. He had been fighting the idea all morning, but he was out making up his mind. That obstinacy that kept him battering at her would keep him on a straight course once he had made his decision. A straight course out of her life.

When she wasn't explaining her entries to Mrs Washington, Barbara busied herself with the everyday work of running the office. She fended off calls from a novelty salesman who wanted to sell them book matches and ballpoint pens emblazoned with the firm's advertisement. She agreed, in the company name, to sponsor five under-priviledged children on a trip to the circus.

Every time a car slowed as it came down the street, she looked up, knowing the sound of the Jeep's engine too well to think it was Chuck, yet still hoping.

The laundry service delivered his denim work clothes and she took them into his office, opening the cupboard to put them away. That was when she noticed the absence of his golf clubs.

'You louse,' she growled and plopped the clothing, still wrapped in a brown-paper bundle, on the shelf.

Another plan shot, she thought as she went back to her desk. She had counted on his remaining in the office, allowing her time with him as a counter-balance against the romantic atmosphere that would surround Sandy. Even that was being taken from her.

In an attempt to keep away the frustration, she worked at top speed, finishing even the filing before the hands of the clock rounded on four-thirty. She still looked up at the sounds of the passing traffic, but no Jeep, no Chuck. She was just covering the typewriter and wondering what to do with herself for the next half-hour when the phone rang.

She heard his voice, disgustingly happy and light, as he asked if there had been any news from Samuels.

She replied in the negative, thinking how glamorous was the sound of tinkling ice in the background, how beautiful the low laughter sounded as it travelled from some unseen lips through the phone he held. Probably Sandy. She took a perverse pleasure in deciding it sounded artificial and deliberately cultured.

'Why don't you get out of there?' Chuck suggested. 'No point in sitting around. See you in the morning.'

'See you then,' Barbara replied, hanging up the phone. She was glad they had not talked longer. He might have heard her disappointment.

'But why should I get out of here?' she asked herself. Going home wasn't fun when she had to go alone. He had spent so much time at her place, evidence of him was all over the flat. The cushion he always put on the end of the coffee-table to prop his feet on was still in its place.

The new regulations manual he brought over and

forgot was still on the small table in the hall. Barbara left it there, knowing it was an extra copy that he planned to take to his place when he remembered it.

To get her mind off him, she would read. But she didn't have anything new. She could peruse *Mediterranean Magic* again. Since she knew the story, maybe she could pick out a few details pertinent to her situation.

She checked the desk, the filing-cabinet, in the drawers and her handbag. She couldn't find the book anywhere.

CHAPTER THREE

BARBARA went home on Monday night, knowing she was going to be miserable because Chuck was out with Sandy. She was. She worked for it; she deserved it. As if determined to punish herself because Chuck was seeing Sandy, she wandered around the room, knocking the cushion off the coffee-table, then putting it back. She made a sandwich and decided to have a beer with it, but the beer didn't taste the same without Chuck there to tell her how good it was. She moped about it for a while, and when she wore out all her misery in that direction, she looked around for something else to be unhappy about.

When she caught sight of herself in her mental mirror she was disgusted. Deciding she could better use her time, she picked up an old copy of a fashion magazine and looked at the models. After making doubly sure the door was locked, she tried some of the poses, but the second time she almost fell off a chair trying to look languid, she gave it up. Obviously those women in the magazine were propped up by something invisible to the camera, and if she could hold the pose, she would certainly be limited in her actions. Dinner would end up in her nonchalant lap.

She put the magazine down, wishing that last fate on Sultry Sandy, and went to bed early. Resuming her pout, she decided she wouldn't be able to sleep, and even if she did, she'd have nightmares, but even her nature turned perverse and she slept all night.

When Barbara arrived at work on Tuesday, Chuck was whistling in his office. His happiness spelled trouble

for Barbara's hopes, so with a sigh she put her handbag
on the filing-cabinet and sat down to open the mail.
When he entered her office he looked as pleased as he
sounded, and he certainly knew the time of day.

'Good morning,' he said as he strode through the
short hall and crossed to the outside door. 'Beautiful
morning this morning.'

'For some people,' Barbara answered shortly, pulling
the cover off her typewriter. Until she finished with the
mail there was nothing to type, but she was suddenly
unequal to facing his high spirits.

'Well, it should certainly be a good day for you.
You're as beautiful as the day. I like that hair-style, and
why I'd kick about seeing a pair of shapely legs, I don't
know.'

Barbara swung around, doing a creditable job of
languishing in the chair by using one foot under the edge
of the desk to keep her balance. She gave him a high-
fashion look.

"What are you after? I didn't ask for a raise, and I
don't care how you flatter me, I'm not driving a truck.'

His face turned serious as he stepped over to the desk
and leaned towards her. Before she knew his intention,
he had captured her left hand in his. He turned it gently,
looking at the palm, then at the manicured nails.

'Who would ask such a thing of so delicate and
beautiful a little hand?' His eyes looked into hers. The
golden lights of his mood sent a warming glow from her
head to her toes. Now she knew the meaning of a
thousands wings, fluttering inside her. 'To misuse this
fragile beauty would be to desecrate the altar of loveli-
ness—' he abruptly dropped her hand and stood back as
if proud of himself. 'How was that?'

Thinking he was making fun of her again, Barbara
whirled around in her chair, and turned to the type-

writer, hoping she could prevent herself from throwing it at him.

'That's the poorest excuse for flattery I've ever heard,' she snapped.

'Damn—' he grunted. If the disappointment in his voice was feigned, he was doing a good job of acting. 'And I worked on that too.'

The door slammed behind him, but Barbara didn't turn around. She sat for a few moments, her fingers playing over the keyboard of the electric typewriter, though the switch wasn't on, and she accomplished nothing. It was just as well, she thought. Her message was frustration, too deep to be recorded on paper. And she had only herself to blame for it, she decided. Sandy had to be the reason for his high spirits. His flattery of Barbara was like a kick in the stomach.

She turned back to finish opening the mail when she realised there was unusual activity in the yard. A strange truck had pulled into the parking lot, loaded with various kinds of equipment and pulling a trailer on which a paving-roller was lashed. Chuck meant it when he said he was going to have the drive and yard repaved. He certainly wasted no time, she thought.

She started the coffee-maker and returned to her desk, planning her projects for the day. But as she glanced out of the window, something else caught her attention. Chuck was standing with one man, pointing out particular spots in the drive, and the two of them appeared to be discussing what should be done. But behind them, three other fellows were looking at Chuck, exchanging meaningful glances and grinning.

Were they laughing at him? Barbara didn't like that at all. What could be so funny? She left the desk and walked over to the door just as Chuck turned, pointing out cracked places in the pavement. Then Barbara saw what struck the other men as so funny.

Sticking out of his back pocket, and almost ready to fall, was a book. She recognised the two figures on the cover, and even if she couldn't read the title from the office, she knew it was her copy of *Mediterranean Magic*. She dashed out, hurrying to where Chuck stood with the paving contractor. Barbara interrupted the conversation without a twinge of conscience.

'Oh, Mr Ingram, thank you for finding my book! I thought I had lost it. You are so thoughtful.'

Chuck looked blank for a moment. Then his face froze. Slowly he reached behind him and removed the paperback from his pocket.

'Uh—yes, Miss Lewis—you—uh—dropped it this morning when you were crossing the yard.'

Back in the office, she put the book in her purse and looked out of the window again. Outside, Chuck was standing with his feet apart, hands on his hips. In his embarrassment, he was playing the bravado bit to the hilt.

She stacked the advertisements and almost threw the business mail in the waste-paper basket as she wondered why he had her book. She did not drop it in the yard. The last time she had seen it had been during their argument the morning before. When Mrs Washington, the accountant came in dropping things, Chuck had been holding it. He had tossed the book on the corner of her desk and stooped to catch the tax forms.

Her eyes opened in surprise. He would have had to come back to her desk to get it. He hasn't picked it up to give back—when he left the office, *he took it with him!* Why? she wondered. To read? No, she couldn't accept that. He probably picked it up, intending to leave it on the desk, and walked out with it in his hand. Chuck could be absent-minded at times. But she was going to tease him anyway, pretending she thought he'd read it.

She sat back and crossed her arms. 'Oh buddy, are you going to pay for that,' she murmured, her blue eyes lighting with mischief. 'After the way you treated me, I'll never let you live it down.'

When he came back into the office, his expression was wary. He knew she was lying in wait. The way his eyes kept travelling to the windows showed his second fear. The men working on the paving might overhear their conversation and he was playing it safe.

She had no intention of humiliating him, but he had to pay. Her eyes spoke all she wanted to impart. They narrowed but the humour peeked out as she let him know he had some nerve taking her book after the attitude he had taken about romances in general, and that one in particular.

Who, me? his green eyes flickered in feigned surprise. *I just found it*, he shrugged, taking refuge in the excuse she had given the paving contractor.

You swiped my book, and I won't forget it, she glowered at him, not hiding the amusement.

'I just bet you won't,' Chuck said, putting his opinion into words as he retreated to the safety of the parking lot where all he had to dodge was hot asphalt and a paving-roller.

For the second day in a row he left during the morning. He had changed out of his denims and wore his best business suit when he left, so she guessed he was with Sandy. The mail had brought no emergencies, the phone was quiet, and the day had dragged interminably.

The paving contractor had dug up several cracked spots, filled them, put down a thick, black, gleaming surface and left just before three o'clock. Barbara was trying to wish away the next two hours when Chuck came strolling in.

'Fancy driveway,' he commented as he shut the outside door. 'We now look substantial and successful.'

'We are absolutely heroic,' Barbara remarked. She had been waiting all day to use that line.

Chuck didn't answer. He slid into the chair by the philodendron and grinned at her. She tensed as he reached towards the plant again, but he was gentle as he brushed some dust off the leaves.

'I've got to hand it to you, you got me out of that one,' he said.

'Oh, you could have managed that by yourself,' Barbara said, determined not to let him cajole her out of her rights. 'But for you to walk off with that book after the way you lit into me—' she paused. She should have rehearsed her retorts. Nothing she could think up on the spur of the moment would quite get across her opinion of his actions.

Then Chuck turned serious. 'I got to thinking about your idea. The more I consider it, the better it gets.'

'What?' Barbara asked, not wanting to believe what she heard.

'These additions you say you're adding to your life. You're right in what you're doing. So I'm a truck driver. That doesn't mean I can't be anything else I want. I don't have to make a religion out of an eighteen-wheeler and a CB radio. There's a lot of stuff out there to be enjoyed. Why should I limit myself?'

'I thought you decided you wanted to be you,' Barbara countered, not liking this attitude at all.

'But you were right,' he argued. 'You said you didn't have to be phony to broaden your scope, well, I don't either. I don't think it would kill me to know the names of a few good wines—to appreciate a good scotch, maybe brandy.'

'You don't like wine,' Barbara objected. 'And the last I heard, you compared brandy to lighter fluid.'

'Well, why *don't* I like them?' he looked indignant. 'Don't people acquire new tastes?'

'I suppose it's partly education, just like learning to type,' Barbara agreed, floored by the new Chuck. She had no illusions about his change of viewpoint. She had hoped he would talk himself out of it, but he was going to try to become what Sandy wanted.

'That's what I thought,' he said, smiling placidly. 'Why don't you make us a reservation—say—at the Bullion Room for Friday night, and let's give it a try.'

'What about Sandy?' One day Barbara was going to bite off her wild tongue, but it was too late after she had asked the question.

'She was only in town for a couple of days, on her way to Italy. She'll be back in ten weeks.' The light in his eyes said he had cause to look forward to her return. In the meantime, he was going to educate himself to what she wanted in a man, and he planned on having Barbara help him. That was too much. If she lost him to Sandy, that was bad enough, but she didn't have to put in time on Sandy's team.

'So, I've been thinking—' Chuck leaned back, crossing his arms over his chest. 'You want to put on some polish, and a little chipping of the rough edges wouldn't do me any harm. We could work on it together. Then maybe we'd both get what we want.'

Barbara looked down at the blank pad on her desk, not knowing how to answer him. She couldn't tell him the outcome he suggested was impossible. They would be working for opposite goals. He for Sandy, Barbara for him. Someone had to lose. She dredged up alternative excuses.

'It would never work. We'd be the blind leading the

blind,' she struggled to think of any excuse to give her objections weight. 'My idea was to start slowly, grow slowly, be sure of my footing—you want a crash course.' A devilish idea struck her. 'You could take a class,' she suggested slyly.

Chuck nodded thoughtfully, but she knew he had not caught her meaning. When he did he sat up with a jerk. His eyes narrowed. Barbara was reminded of a large animal as his muscles tensed with wariness. She wasn't sure whether his instinct was to spring away or attack.

'What did you mean by that?'

Her own instinct for survival was suddenly foremost. Her intention had been to plant the idea of a charm school in his mind, knowing he would be revolted by the idea. Not that she knew of such a place for adults. But planting the thought was one thing. Actually suggesting it to him was another.

'I—uh—I'm not sure,' she stammered. 'Maybe in wines?—maybe in—' she let the words trail off, wishing she hadn't tried to be so smart.

'No,' Chuck said. He was decisive as he leaned forward, his elbows on his spread knees. 'No, I think we can teach each other if we work at it.'

'It's a dumb idea,' Barbara wanted to stop the words and couldn't. 'You said so yesterday—I can see that now. I was just defending it because—'

'Because you were right, and you should have,' he interrupted. 'I was fighting it because I needed to see the point and didn't want to.'

'But why should you? *You* were right, you are your own person, too strong, too valuable to change for someone else's whim. Well, so am I. I don't want someone who only sees the outside—' Barbara stopped. She was having a problem keeping her foot out of her mouth. That particular remark was hitting too close to criticism of Sandy. It was also, she acknowledged, a close description of Chuck.

He missed both similarities as he sat energetically shaking his head.

'You're not talking about strength or pride, that's ego speaking. I think, if you truly love—' he paused, his eyes on his distant thought, and Barbara's heart wrenched for the vulnerability in his strong-boned face. 'If you really love someone you want them to take a certain pride in you—a never-ending pride.' He looked back at her. 'But if a person is willing to accept the responsibility of another person's love, they shouldn't begrudge a little effort to keep the other person happy.'

Barbara let her head drop. She stared at the litter of papers on her desk and knew the battle was lost. He was negating ego, but he was speaking out of pride. She had opened a door that had gone previously unnoticed by him, but now that he had looked through it, he was determined to make that foreign land his own.

'Call the Bullion Room and make a reservation,' he said as he stood up. 'We'll dress for it, order fancy wines and try out our new status.'

'Do you know how to choose a wine?' she asked.

His chin went up as he shoved his hands in his pockets and strutted across the room. 'I bought a book. I'll take another look at it before Friday. You know, I'm surprised. I still remember some of my high-school French.' He reached for the door and turned back. 'Just one thing—'

'Yes?' The change in his tone of voice brought Barbara's head up.

'You'll have to hold me on course. I might see the sense in it, but I'll be fighting it all the way.'

He left the office and Barbara watched as he crossed the yard to the mechanics' shed. He was going to do it,

she thought. Reluctantly she took the telephone directory from the drawer and looked up the number of the
restaurant he suggested.

Three large private parties had booked the Bullion
Room for Friday evening. As she hung up the phone,
her first thought was to just give him the message and
hope the idea would die there. But Chuck was determined. If she didn't make an effort to help him, he might
find another partner for his scheme. The possibility
made her cringe, but what weighed on her conscience
was the knowledge that he depended upon her to help
him, and he believed he was helping her. With a sigh she
turned the pages, looking at the advertisements for
other restaurants.

Her gaze stopped at the Chez la Jouissance. He did
say he remembered his high-school French, didn't he?
Then why not? Several times when driving past the
famous restaurant she had gazed at it wistfully. Chuck's
confidence in his new role would be bolstered. She
picked up the phone again.

She intended to tell Chuck about the change in plans,
but business intervened. A new client with an emergency shipment caused Chuck to change professional hats.
In half an hour he had changed clothes, thrown a flight
bag into the back of the new GM diesel and was on his
way to pick up a shipment bound for San Francisco. He
was due back Friday afternoon.

Normally, Barbara took pride in finishing all her work
and taking care of the filing before leaving work, but not
that Friday. She had been alone in the office for two
days, and Chuck, when he returned from his trip,
had checked the mail and left again. At a quarter
past four, she stacked the files and locked the door,
hoping no important calls would come in before closing
time.

As she walked out to her car she consoled herself with the thought that she was in an all-out but undeclared war. She let a sly grin play across her features. Her battle would be conducted on the principles of guerrilla warfare, since neither Chuck nor Sandy knew she was in the fight. At least no one would be expecting her attack, she decided, and she was going home to prepare her ammunition.

The Volks, when she started it, behaved perfectly, but a block from the office it started sputtering again.

'Darn, I forgot to tell Chuck about your colic,' she told the car. She wondered if she should take it back to the office and decided against it. If they were going to have a beautiful evening, Chuck didn't need to wear himself out working on the car.

Three blocks from the office, she suddenly pulled to the curb. Chuck wanted to develop a sophistication in his alcoholic tastes, did he? As she stepped out of the car she tried to remember the name of that stuff—was it liquor, wine, liqueur? she wasn't sure. But from an old friend's description of something she had tried, it sounded perfect for their safari into the jungles of sophistication. She strolled into the off licence and looked around. Most of the names could have been written in Latin or Greek, for all she knew about them. That sparked her mind. Greek—whatever it was, Louise had said it was Greek.

'Ouzo,' the grinning clerk said when she gave a disjointed description of what she wanted.

He went to a shelf and picked out a bottle of unoffending clear liquor.

'Sort of—' at a loss for words, Barbara mimicked Louise's pantomimed description by fanning herself with one hand and blowing through pursed lips as if she had bitten into a red pepper.

'That's it,' the clerk affirmed and rang up the sale as Barbara took out her wallet.

At home she relaxed in a leisurely bath, washed, dried and curled her hair, and spent a delicious afternoon just taking care of her fingernails, experimenting with her new make-up and choosing an outfit from her array of new clothes.

She stood in front of the mirror, holding up one dress and then another. Her handbag stood to one side, open where she had emptied part of the contents on the polished walnut dresser top. Her copy of *Mediterranean Magic* cast a double image as it was reflected back, flanked by her favourite lipstick, and a small cosmetic case. Damon on the front of the cover seemed to be critical.

Barbara told herself she was letting her imagination run away with her, but the more she gazed at the green and white silk, the more she seemed to see a frown in the book hero's eyes.

'Okay, that one's out,' Barbara said as she hung the dress back in the cupboard.

The next outfit she took out, a mauve and cream striped sundress with a jacket, looked better. Her eyes were a particular blue that mauve seemed to intensify, and she had *loved* the subtle accents the wide bands of colour added to her figure.

Now Damon looked approving. Melissa seemed to be wearing the frown. Barbara looked hesitantly from the book to the mirror, where she held the dress up in front of her and back again at the book. She raised her chin and threw the dress on the bed.

'Let's not fight about it,' she said to the cover, and turned to find suitable accessories.

By the time Chuck rang the bell she was ready, though he was far earlier than he needed to be. That was one of his quirks, and she was accustomed to it. That night she had counted on it.

When she opened the door, he gave her his usual cursory glance, as if he were only making sure he had not rung the wrong bell. But suddenly his eyes jerked back to her, a slight frown added a crease between his brows.

'I didn't bring my brass knuckles,' he said curtly.

'Hunh?' Barbara was a little too confused to be elegant in her reply.

'The way you look tonight, I may have to fight off half the men in town,' Chuck said as he walked around her and into the flat.

She resisted the urge to slam the door. After closing it, she stared at the blank, white painted surface, seeing in the unmarked smoothness her future with Chuck. Even when he complimented her, he didn't think of her in terms of himself. She might appeal strongly to some other man, but not to him.

She squared her shoulders and turned back into the flat. The fight wasn't over yet.

At the end of the short hallway she paused. Chuck was standing in the dining-room. The overhead light, which she had dimmed early, made a golden aura of his sunbleached curls. His eyes, shaded as he looked down at the bottle he was holding, were hidden. In the half shadow, his face was caught in its planes, giving him a slight air of mystery, a subtle fascination that caught at Barbara's heart.

He certainly looked the part of the sophisticated man around town. She had not seen that particular suit. The fit spoke of tailoring, murmuring with a British accent, displaying his compact frame with an elegance that hinted at power beneath the well sewn seams. The soft grey colour carried just a hint of smoke blue and brought out the same colour in his eyes.

Barbara wondered if she too might need those brass knuckles to keep her escort for the evening. What *were* brass knuckles, anyway?

'What's this?' Chuck asked, holding up the bottle.

'Ouzo.'

'I can see that.' Just a trace of impatience. 'Why is it here?'

Barbara felt a shiver of worry and discarded it. 'We were going to experience the elite, remember? The hero in the book drank it. I thought we might give it a try—just a start on our education.'

Chuck's suspicions cleared, leaving him interested. 'Good. We'll toast our venture. Need ice?'

'You open the bottle,' she handed it back to him. 'I'll get the makings.'

While Chuck watched, Barbara put the ice cubes in the glasses and poured the clear Greek liquor over them. She added what she thought was the proper amount of water. As she agitated the drinks with a glass stirrer, the clear liquid turned a milky white.

Chuck eyed the drinks and looked up at Barbara warily. 'Will it start smoking?'

'Of course not,' she retorted, but she would have refused a wager on it.

They traded two more glances before Chuck took a deep breath, reached out and picked up a glass. He sniffed it.

'Smells like candy,' he said, a little reassured. He carried both drinks into the living-room and put them on the coffee-table. When he put them down, he removed his cushion from the end of the table and put it back on the loveseat. Tonight he was more formal in his attitude than in his attire. He stood until Barbara took her place and sat by her. She felt strong misgivings over his demeanour. What good did it do her to dress to the hilt if he were going to play Lord Stuffy?

'Does smell like candy,' he repeated as he handed her a glass. He raised his own and touched hers with a clink of camaraderie. 'To our goals,' he said.

'To our goals,' Barbara repeated, taking pleasure in the knowledge that they were speaking of two different endings. 'Here's to the candy in life,' she added and took a drink from her glass.

Candied kerosene! she thought as she fought for breath. Did mauve complement bulging eyes? Chuck's had widened slightly, and when he blinked she noticed a new brightness. He swallowed three times before he spoke.

'Very—Greek,' he managed in hardly more than a whisper.

'Puts h-hair on your chest,' Barbara's reply was slightly indistinct, she was still trying to get her tongue out of its self-defensive knot and get her breathing back in order. 'L-look what it does for Greek men. Makes them shipping magnates and all sorts of stuff.'

Chuck was staring into his glass as if he expected it to house a war. He mumbled, and Barbara thought she heard, 'Remind me to sell my trucks.'

'Did you say something?'

He looked up startled. 'I said good luck—good luck you found it—quite a—uh—quite an experience, this ouzo.'

'It's supposed to get better as you get used to it,' Barbara said, eyeing the glass. Was it worth it? she wondered. Was anything worth it? She had hoped for something so unpalatable he would be forced to give up his plan. It wasn't supposed to have that effect on her.

'I doubt it,' Chuck mumbled, but when she turned to look at him in query, he changed his words. 'I'm ready for another experiment, how about it?'

She shook her head. He went back to the dining-room and she leaned back on the sofa, thinking over the failure in this step of her plan. She let her head fall back on the cushions and closed her eyes as she wondered how to sway his determination . . .

She was still considering when the movement of the couch warned her of his return. She opened her eyes to see his face only inches from hers.

'You okay?' His eyes were searching her face. He was so close. The dark fringe of his lashes curled until they lay against his tanned, dark-textured skin. His hair had fallen forward a bit, a few strands of bleached gold lay on his forehead.

'Beautiful,' Barbara whispered.

Chuck pulled back, his grin only partially hiding his surprise. 'What?'

Barbara closed her eyes, hoping by hiding the sight of him she could shut away her embarrassment. 'I'm helping you,' she forced the words, bringing them out lightly. 'You're supposed to be a hero, remember? The hero never misses an opportunity to win his lady-love by making flattering remarks.'

'I thought that guy in the book did pretty well with insults.' Chuck's voice sounded hollow. Barbara peeked between her lashes to see him take a drink from his filled glass and shudder. Maybe her idea was working.

'But he started off with complimentary remarks,' Barbara insisted. 'You have to pet the kitty-cat to get it close enough to kick.'

'Then I guess I had better get in practice if I ever decide on cruelty to animals.' He set the glass on the table and leaned close again. 'But I wouldn't say you're beautiful.'

No, you'd keep that for Sandy, Barbara thought with a

pang as he lifted a tress of her hair.

'I think I'd ask about the magic weavers who spun dreams into hair—' for emphasis he let it fall in a shower of strands. Then with gentle fingers he brushed it back from her face. He traced her eyebrows, his feather touch sensitising the skin on her cheeks. 'I'd be curious about the sky that got into your eyes, and how they capture the starlight in the middle of the day.'

Forgetting the game, Barbara stared up at him, enraptured. She had no idea he could be so fanciful, so flattering. Her heart was pounding, every part of her demanded she reciprocate, but she held herself back out of fear. Was he seeing her or Sandy? The humour had disappeared from his face, his eyes had darkened with intensity. His fingers explored her ears, her cheeks, rounded her chin and came up to her mouth. She waited in anticipation as he stared at her lips.

'There are no words,' he murmured and lowered his mouth to hers.

His kiss was gentle, more exploratory than urgent. A feather-touch, moving on unknown territory, savouring, appreciative of what it found. His tongue travelled the outer edges and finding no resistance became more sure. It parted her lips and played against the softer more sensitive skin. When he drew back she wanted to hold him, to keep him from going, but knew now was not the time.

When she opened her eyes she was surprised at the look on his face. He was visibly shaken, surprised at his own reaction. She took pleasure in his puzzled look. Her first skirmish had been successful.

Be careful, she warned herself. *It won't help to win the battles and lose the war*. If she shook him up too much, he might shy off. Chuck had a clearly defined sense of honour, and believing himself committed to Sandy, he would not want Barbara's heart just as a trophy, she knew.

'Well-ll,' she murmured. 'The description in the book read better than that.'

Chuck had picked up his glass. He almost dropped it on the table. His eyes said he couldn't believe it. Slowly he turned so that he was facing her. The ice he levered into his question lost its effectiveness in his incredulity.

'Exactly what was wrong with that kiss?'

'That's not tonight's lesson,' Barbara said lightly as she picked up her glass and tried the ouzo again. She shuddered.

'Was that the liquor, or me?' Chuck demanded.

'We'll work on both,' Barbara said lightly as she picked up the glasses and carried them into the kitchen. Chuck followed her, bringing the bottle of ouzo, the pitcher of cold water and the ice bucket.

'I can kiss just as well as anyone else,' he insisted.

'Maybe just as well, but certainly not heroic,' she said as she kept her hands out of his sight while she crossed her fingers. It was sacrilege to malign that kiss, but she wouldn't tell him that. She rinsed out the glasses as an excuse not to face him. She knew she couldn't hide her smile. 'And while we're on the subject, those compliments were really old hat.'

'You're saying I can't do anything right? Exactly what do you expect?'

'A hero! Maybe it's just because you're hungry. The reservation is at eight, so we'd better get started.'

In the hall she picked up her purse and waited for Chuck to open the door. He had been stalking behind her, his eyes dark with frustration and anger. Now he stepped around her and jerked at the knob.

She sailed past him and strolled down the hall. He caught up with her and by the time they had reached the front entrance of the building he had found his tongue again.

'We're going to take this up later,' he growled. 'I'll tell *you* something, *Heroine*—you insult Mr Wonderful like that and you'll never get him hooked. And I'm going to make you take those remarks back—that's something I'm not putting up with—I can kiss as well as anyone *you've* ever known! When I get a chance I'll *show* you—'

Barbara made no answer. Let him talk himself out, she thought. Chuck usually kept his word, and she was looking forward to it.

CHAPTER FOUR

'I'M sorry, I didn't know what else to do,' Barbara said that evening as they watched the commissionaire drive the VW away. Behind her the door of Chez la Jouissance looked strangely forbidding.

'Hey, it was a great idea.' Chuck took her arm and guided her in. His words were reassuring. His tone, deliberately light, warned her he was not exactly pleased with her choice in restaurants.

The commissionaire had raised his brows at the battered Volkswagen, but once inside, they had nothing to be ashamed of. Chuck's suit bore the stamp of the city's best tailor. In his work clothes, his tanned face and sunbleached hair gave the impression of a man who laboured hard, but in the dark blue suit he could have stepped off a yacht or a tennis court. She had often noticed how easily he handled people, but as they strolled into the restaurant and she saw him in surroundings so different from the usual, she realised there was about him the unmistakable air of a man who commanded. No trace of the ex-truck-driver showed through. Barbara was seeing him now from Sandy's viewpoint. He was not dismayed by circumstances.

At least he gave the impression of not being dismayed. Once they were seated and he looked over the menu, he raised his gaze to meet Barbara's. His mouth pursed. His eyes travelled with deliberate casualness around the room, checking to see if he could be overheard. Then he leaned forward slightly.

'There's a *lot* more to this French than I remember. I

thought they'd have English subtitles.'

Barbara had let her eyes travel over the menu, but depending on Chuck to order for her, she had admired the strange-looking words with the half-mind of a tourist taking in the scenery of a strange country. *Oui, m'sieur* and *non* was her total knowledge of the language.

'What difference does it make?' she answered in a voice pitched as low as his. 'Just sound as if you know what you're doing. We'll eat whatever you order.'

Chuck looked dubious. 'How do you feel about cherry pie on your shrimp?'

'My favourite dish,' Barbara assured him. 'Just remember, all Europeans are supposed to think Americans are eccentric or crazy.'

'Just *sound* like I know what I'm doing, hunh?' His little-boy grin was masking his worry.

'Should work,' she answered, sure that Chuck could pull it off.

The waiter had retreated to his station, but at Chuck's nod he came forward at once.

'*Dos v-rin-ce—no-boush*—and—*ferm—mandataire,*' Chuck said as he closed the menu.

The first stab of worry hit Barbara. She might not know French, but *dos* was Spanish for two. The two was fine. The Spanish bothered her a little.

'*Oui monsieur,* but—'

'That's all for now, we'll order dinner later,' Chuck said with a nod of dismissal. The waiter hesitated a moment, then shrugged and walked away.

All in all, Barbara was pleased. Maybe two was the same in both languages.

'Marvellous,' she said. 'You sound like a world traveller.'

Chuck accepted the compliment as if it were his due.

'We could be making waves over nothing. I mean, what's the big deal?'

Barbara nodded, but her heart wasn't in her enthusiasm. He was right, he only needed to open his mind. He was certainly capable of going anywhere, of doing anything. To tell him that would put an end to his efforts, and probably put him out of her romantic life. She decided she wasn't going to be that honest. Her only chance to fight Sandy was to stick it out with him.

The candle-light made his eyes shine a dreamy greenish gold. Little strands of gold coursed through the darker hair and seemed to move with the flicker of the flames. The moving glow gave the planes of his face new depth. Barbara knew his mind too well to believe he was thinking about her. He was envisaging Sandy sitting in her place. She dropped her eyes and watched his hands as they absently caressed the linen tablecloth, the silver, the bases of the crystal stemware.

He loved beautiful things. He would soon become accustomed to the best, because his nature leaned that way. No wonder he wanted Sandy, Barbara thought. Sandy would have known what he ordered.

Sandy would have known, but she certainly didn't, Babs thought. She stared down at the bowl the waiter set in front of her and decided she was out of her element completely. She didn't know what that clear liquid with the floating rose petals was in French, but in English, that was a finger bowl. As the waiter laid a small towel by the side of it, she knew she was right.

Chuck's look of startled chagrin warned her he expected something different. And the waiter had further unwelcome news for him.

'I beg your pardon, *m'sieur*, but the chef informs me he does not have the recipe for "a steady agent"—is it a drink?'

Across the table, Chuck's gaze met hers.

His said she *had* to pick a place without subtitles.

Barbara's said she was sorry.

His wanted to know if she had any more bright ideas.

Chuck picked up the menu again. He took some time looking it over. Then he held it so the waiter could see his selection.

'We'll have that—' he paused to look warily at the waiter. 'If it's food.'

The waiter smiled and nodded sympathetically as he turned away. When he was out of hearing, Chuck stuck one finger in the bowl in front of him and idly stirred a rose petal. For a moment he didn't look up at Barbara. She could not allow him to feel like a fool, even if she sounded like one.

'That was thoughtful of you. You're adding a new dimension to the consideration of a hero.' She busied herself wetting her fingers and drying them on the towel. 'So convenient, so much luxury. You're a constant surprise.' She was grateful when his face relaxed and she knew he felt better. Just how much could she say about a finger bowl?

Chuck's enthusiasm for his new lifestyle had been dampened by the floating rose petals, and Barbara was not sure whether to be glad or sorry. She wanted him to give up this far-fetched plan, but the decision must be his, he must not fail. She was striving for a way to give him back his confidence when he suddenly raised his chin and grinned. He picked up a fork and bounced it between a thumb and forefinger as he used it for emphasis.

'You know, I've been thinking about that book—that character didn't try to go everywhere and do everything. Maybe that's the solution. Stick with your strong points.'

'Good idea,' she agreed, trying to build up some

enthusiasm. Her emotions ran the gambit of two. When he was down she was worried; when he was up she was afraid of losing him.

Chuck was feeling much better by the time their dinner arrived. Barbara looked at the plate and made a mental note of the arrangement. The balance of the food on the plate, the colours, the textures, all added to a beautiful picture as if they had been presented with gifts too perfectly wrapped to disturb. She licked her lips in anticipation, but first she just wanted to admire it.

A nasty little stab of resentment struck her. Sandy probably gave a lot of thought to the arrangement of food on a plate—that was, if Sandy could cook. Barbara considered the dish in front of her. The carrots were a beautiful orange. The broccoli was topped by white-gold hollandaise that promised to be delightful. Barbara tested it by taking a small amount on her fork and letting her tongue savour it. Her eyes rolled up, giving vent to her ecstasy. The baked potatoes were duchesse, re-placed in the jacket, and garnished with herbs she didn't recognise.

Chuck brought her out of her reverie. 'I like baby carrots,' he murmured.

Barbara nodded in agreement and gazed at her plate again. The pleasure slowly began to ebb. Why did he have to mention baby? The small, beautifully golden quail were too reminiscent of baby chickens. Baby chickens, all covered with yellow fluff before they started getting their feathers. She was being silly, she knew, but the image of pert little biddies, running along behind mother hen would not go away.

'What's the matter?' Chuck mumbled, hastily swal-lowed and repeated more clearly. 'Don't tell me it isn't good. This is fantastic.'

Barbara raised her gaze to his, then dropped her eyes,

focusing on the glass of wine. 'When I was a kid, Mother used to complain about my Easter basket.'

'So? What has that to do with dinner?'

'I never ate those little marshmallow chickens—the yellow ones. They looked like babies.'

She looked up to see if he understood. He was frowning; his gaze travelled from her face to her plate and cleared. He saw her problem and smiled with sympathy. He could be amazingly sympathetic at times.

'That's quail,' he reassured her. 'They're supposed to be small, that's why they gave you two.'

'They look like little chickens,' Barbara insisted. 'When you were a kid, didn't anyone give you a dyed baby chick at Easter? Mine was pink. Yours had to be blue.'

'Green, called him Robin Hood,' Chuck corrected her. 'And those birds on your plate are quail. They're probably great, now *try* them.'

How could he *look* so understanding and be so heartless? Barbara knew she was talking herself into being foolish, and having him point it out just made it worse. He should have said something soothing. But why should he? She was being so childish she could almost feel the pigtails down her back, but knowing it didn't help. Her frustration with herself found a target in him.

'I bet you *ate* your little green chicken!' she accused him.

Chuck's head came up, insulted. Then he laughed aloud. The other diners looked around and smiled as if vicariously sharing another's good time. Chuck leaned forward, pointed a piece of French bread at her for emphasis.

'When I was ten I didn't eat *anything* green—spinach, broccoli, *or* chickens. And Robin Hood grew up to be the scourge of the neighbourhood. He died of old age. Take a better man than me to eat *him*.'

He turned his attention to his plate again, and Barbara did the same. The gorgeous arrangement no longer looked appetising. She raised her eyes and saw the waiter walking across the floor to another table. He was probably delivering another dish of succulent infants.

You abetter of cannibals, she flung the silent insult in his direction. Across the table, Chuck was picking at his food. He had spent part of the day working on one of the trucks. After hard labour he was always ravenous, yet he had stopped after only a few bites. Barbara was suddenly worried. Maybe he didn't feel well.

'I thought you liked your dinner,' Barbara prodded.

'It's okay,' his answer was short.

'Then what's the matter? Why aren't you eating?'

His eyes had gone grey. Not a good sign. He was irritated. 'You *had* to start that bit about little chickens.'

'But you know it's quail.'

'And about the size of Robin Hood when he sneaked in the house and pecked the sequins off Mama's evening bag.' With a sigh, he pushed his plate away. 'Why couldn't you keep your thoughts to yourself? I *was* enjoying it.'

'I'm sorry,' Barbara did the same, regretting the evening, the entire idea. She was being stupid, she knew it. Resolutely she pulled the plate back and picked up her fork. But no way was she going to bite that baby chicken, even if it was a quail.

'I can't do it,' she moaned. 'I know I'm foolish, but I've talked myself into it, and now I'm stuck with it.'

'You didn't have to stick me with it,' Chuck complained and signalled for the bill.

'The dinner is not satisfactory, *monsieur*?' From the expression on the waiter's face, no other patrons in the history of Chez la Jouissance had so completely spurned the food. He stood disbelieving, his eyes wide with apprehension.

'Perfectly satisfactory,' Chuck answered shortly. 'Please bring the bill.'

'But *monsieur*, if something was wrong—'

Chuck proved he was a hero of substance. No brows would have been raised with more supercilious arrogance. He pronounced each word with clipped formality.

'I don't care to discuss it. The bill, please.'

While they were waiting for the car, Barbara buttoned her thin jacket. The clouds were no longer threatening, they were making a definite promise. The breeze had strengthened to a cold wind.

'You scared that poor waiter to death,' she said.

Chuck gave her a frown. 'What was I supposed to tell him? That we don't eat little animals and carrots that aren't old enough to walk?'

'Don't start with the carrots!' Barbara warned him. 'We've got enough trouble with animals right now. If we start on the vegetables, we'll never eat anything.'

The first spatter of raindrops fell as Chuck pulled the car out of the restaurant's driveway and on to the side street that fronted on the freeway. Half a block further on, the Volkswagen gave a gurgle, a sputter and settled into a buck and jump style of missing.

'What now?' Chuck growled as he tried feeding it more throttle. The hesitation became worse.

'Oh—Little Sadie!' Barbara was dismayed at the behaviour of the car. 'She gave me some trouble a couple of times, but then started running right again. And the missing never was this bad.'

'Why didn't you tell me?'

'It stopped—I meant to mention it but I forgot.'

'Well, next time don't forget. Engines aren't like people, they don't heal themselves. You could have been out somewhere alone, you know.'

'Yes,' Barbara replied. He was telling her something, though he probably didn't realise it. Sandy would be back in town in a few weeks. Then, if Barbara went out in the evenings, she would be alone. But she shouldn't think about that. If she was to stand a chance with Chuck, her mind and energies had to be turned in a positive direction. Direction—where was he going?

'You missed the entrance to the freeway,' she told him.

'I know. I don't think we'd better take Little Sadie out in fast traffic.'

With Chuck at the wheel, Barbara forgot about her car troubles. In fact they seemed to be easing off a bit. Probably because of the way he was driving, she thought. If anything went wrong with the car, he could handle it. Maybe he didn't speak French, but he could talk Volkswagen with the best of them. But did he know the roads in this part of the country? Normally they zipped on and off the big freeways. No one drove along the side roads any more. Many people in San Diego believed the six-to-twelve-lane freeways were the only possible way to cross the city and travel in the surrounding areas.

She opened the glove compartment and took out her map book. The storm had brought on a premature darkness and she had trouble locating their position. Chuck kept turning his head while she searched. Hoping he would not be insulted, she continued to look. Before she found the right page he started laying out his route.

'We'll take Pomerado, I think. Then we'll cut back across the freeway and go down from there,' he said.

'Been some time since I've been out this way. Watch for a turn before too long.'

Barbara murmured her agreement and studied the map in the half-light. She checked the glove compartment and took out the flashlight she always carried, but the car's hesitation, its slight, irregular jumping, made her aim of the bright beam leap about on the map. Every time her eyes focused, the page seemed to be somewhere else.

'That turn should be coming up,' Chuck reminded her as he came out of a wide S-curve.

She saw a double curve on the map and a road going off to the left. 'Take your next left,' she said. A quick glance at the road showed he just had time to put on his signal light. The rain was pouring, preventing them from seeing far ahead.

'I thought I remembered turning to the right,' Chuck said as he headed into the darkness. The road was not as wide, Barbara noticed. She had driven along Pomerado Road a year ago and remembered it being in better condition. But roads deteriorated in California as well as in Iowa. But satisfied that he now knew where he was, she closed the book and put it away.

The rain was coming down harder. In the darkness she could barely see the edge of the road, and in a few minutes even that wasn't visible. The storm drainage was full of mud as though it had washed out a gully somewhere in front of them. In the semicircles of momentary clarity given her by the windscreen wipers, she could see the black, gleaming road, obscured in places by swirls of pale sand-coloured water.

She glanced apprehensively at Chuck. In the dim light from the dashboard she could see his attention to his driving. She was relieved that he wasn't hunched forward, taut with the recognition of a dangerous problem.

He was quiet, all his attention turned to the road. His left hand lightly held the steering-wheel as he skirted the muddy water. His right rested on the gear lever near her left knee and two fingers were stretched out to touch her seat. They tapped lightly on the cording of the upholstery as if he was giving the little car an added assurance that they were a team, and would get through together.

While she was watching him he slowed the car.

'What's the matter?' she asked, slightly frightened.

'Just water running across the road,' he answered, changing into a lower gear. Using the clutch and accelerator in combination, he kept the engine revving at high speed as he drove slowly forward. Waves splashed out from both sides of the car, but it seemed to Barbara as if not more than two inches of water covered the road. From an angle she could see another car approaching. It was coming at a weird direction, she thought.

'Chuck—?' her query was tentative, and cut off by his oath. He had seen the car too, and realised the road turned, but not in time. Barbara felt a sickening lurch as first the front and then the rear wheels went into the ditch. To make matters worse, the oncoming car sent a spray of muddy water completely over the Volkswagen as it sailed by. Even though the windows were up, Barbara ducked.

'The end of a perfect evening,' Chuck said in disgust.

'Where did we go wrong?' Barbara asked. She looked out into the darkness on her side of the car. They weren't on much of an angle, which meant the ditch wasn't too deep. California, like its neighbouring states in the Southwest, could have dangerous washouts, but she knew they weren't in any peril from that direction. Gullies and arroyos crossing the road would be death traps in sudden storms, but in the car lights she could see they were on a mildly sloping hillside.

'We went where the road didn't,' Chuck said flatly. 'It curved to the left, but with this sheet of muddy water covering it—' he let her figure the rest out for herself as he leaned forward and took the flashlight from the glove compartment.

'And another thing,' he said as he straightened. 'This is definitely not Pomerado Road. That car was the only one we've passed.'

'You're saying we're not likely to get any help,' Barbara summarised.

'Right, unless we want to hoof it.'

'You're the one that knows what to do,' Barbara said slowly. 'You make the decision.'

'Have your say now,' Chuck insisted. 'If I walk you walk—I won't leave you here alone. I guess the best thing to do is try to push it out.'

'Okay,' Barbara said, raising one foot to unbuckle her shoe. It was only fair that she should help him. After all, she had told him to make the turn.

'What are you doing?'

'I'm taking off my shoes, I'm not ruining them in that dirty water.'

'You stay in the car. I'll push, you drive it out.'

'I don't know about that,' Barbara argued. 'I'm okay on the road, but I don't do well in ditches.'

'Just do as I tell you,' Chuck growled, taking off his coat. 'We'll make it. VWs' are surefooted little devils.' He opened the door, letting in a lash of rain as he stepped out into the night.

Barbara shivered as she slid into the left-hand seat. She pitied him, out in the cold rain. He suffered through a dreadful evening. She had put him in an embarrassing position with her choice of restaurants, ruined his dinner and then given him bad directions that caused them to end up in a ditch. He was a forbearing person, she thought. One more goof-up on her part, and he would certainly never take *her* out again, Barbara thought.

She pushed in the clutch and dropped the lever into first gear. The engine was sputtering worse than ever, the oil and generator light flashed on and off as the engine nearly stopped. Twice, with her foot still on the clutch, she revved the engine, but the sputters only increased.

I'll never do it, she thought. The sideways tilt of the car, the unfamiliar surroundings, and the dark stormy night made everything seem strange, even usually faithful Little Sadie.

'Okay, take it out,' Chuck shouted. She felt the slight movement of the car as he put his weight against it.

Eyes half closed, her face contorted into a scrunch of wishing, she pressed on the accelerator and let in the clutch. Little Sadie went into shivers and snorts, then suddenly the engine seemed to get where it was going and with a roar the VW snarled out of the ditch and skidded half way around on the road before Barbara got it under control and stopped.

In the illumination of the car lights reflecting off the water, Barbara saw Chuck on his knees in the ditch and just getting to his feet. In a flash she was out of the car, running towards him as he brushed the muddy water off his face.

'Are we late for another reservation?' he yelled.

Barbara stared at him, too miserable to say a word. This was the last straw, she knew. If she didn't get her notice on Monday, he would at least avoid her like the plague after office hours. But she couldn't think about her own problems at the moment. He was chilled to the bone, she could see him trembling. The trembling became a shake. Then the sound of the rain was muted by his roar of laughter. He splashed towards her and dropped an arm about her shoulders. She smiled tremulously up at him, not sure whether he was suffering from an aggravated sense of humour or just losing his mind.

'I think we'd better re-read that book,' he said when he could speak again. 'I don't think we've caught the spirit yet.'

'I'm so sorry,' Barbara murmured as they walked back to the car.

'You shouldn't be,' he said as he led her around the car and opened the door on the passenger's side. 'Just look at what we've learned to avoid. That has to count for something.'

Back in town, Chuck pulled up in front of his flat. He double parked but didn't turn off the engine.

'It won't take me but a minute to change clothes and come down,' he said. 'Drive around the block a couple of times—I'll be right back.'

Barbara had a better idea. Three blocks away she pulled into a drive-in fast food restaurant and ordered hamburgers and french fries. When she pulled up and stopped, sliding over so he could take over the wheel again, the white paper bag was in the back seat by his coat. He had changed into a pair of jeans and a velour shirt. He was through playing hero for the night, she decided. But the soft green shirt brought out colour in those chameleon hazel eyes and added a glow to his suntanned complexion.

Back at her flat, Barbara left Chuck with the bag of hamburgers while she went to change her clothes. Her shoes were ruined, she decided as she removed them. At the moment she wasn't worried about it. Her dress had a streak of mud down the side where she had brushed against Chuck's clothes.

She pulled on a pair of comfortable jeans, slipped into a light yellow sweater and twisted her hair up into a roll since it was still damp and would require drying and curling before it looked decent. After the fiasco of the evening, she wouldn't impress Chuck with a baseball bat, she decided.

In the kitchen the coffee-pot was doing its stuff, the hamburgers were sitting out on plates, and Chuck was mixing water with the ouzo, frowning at it as it changed to a milky white. He looked up as she stopped by the table.

'From now on, I take my education where it's safe,' he said, handing her a glass. 'Here's to no more goof-ups.'

'Here, here, hoy, hoy, and whatever,' Barbara said fervently. She took a sip, gasped and put the glass down quickly. She wasn't quite as fast as Chuck in getting rid of the drink.

'Hamburgers,' Chuck said, picking up a plate and gazing at the bun as if fascinated. 'How old was the cow?'

Barbara arched her brows, picked up a french fry and shook it playfully in his direction. 'Certified thirty-years old, and a public menace. Killed for punitive action, no guilt for eating him.'

Chuck was quiet for a moment as he stared at the burger. 'Are you sure he didn't leave a family of hopeful calves behind, poor little critters, mooing for their ground up papa—'

'You stop that!' Barbara shouted at him as he looked up, his eyes gold with laughter. He was wreaking vengeance on her for spoiling his dinner, but hers had been spoiled too.

'Poor little veal cutlets,' he crooned.

'How are you at wearing your burgers?' she asked, raising her plate an inch off the table. She was having trouble keeping her mouth in a straight firm line. He was going to make her laugh, and he knew it. She gave up her pretence at indignation.

The teasing stopped until they finished eating. Then, while Barbara cleared the table, Chuck carried the drinks into the living-room. When she followed him with the coffee, he was sitting on the sofa, his feet propped on the cushion at the end of the coffee-table. He was immersed in her copy of *Mediterranean Magic*.

'What are you looking for?' Barbara asked as she looked over his shoulder. He seemed dissatisfied, and kept flipping pages.

'We're not going at this right,' Chuck replied. 'If we don't do better the next time, we get another book.'

'Maybe it's just a bad idea,' Barbara ventured. She tried to keep her voice steady, to keep the hope out of it. If he gave up the plan as silly, Sandy would be out of his life a week after she returned from Europe.

'No, we're right in what we're doing,' Chuck said. She wasn't surprised at his attitude. That determination was an integral part of his character, a character she loved, and she would be sorry to see it changed.

Her only hope was for him to see for himself some error that would make him want to drop the scheme. Now, where was the error? she wondered. Maybe she could find it. She gazed at him as he studied the book, a small frown of concentration wrinkling his forehead. The frown deepened. He looked up, scornful. He held the paperback for her to see, open to page one hundred and fifty-nine. With one finger he stabbed at the second paragraph as if he could poke a hole in all the theories of romance.

'That's not a kiss!'
Barbara leaned forward and read:

'Come to me, woman, and learn what a man is,'
Damon snarled and pulled Melissa to him. Her breath
was forced from her by the strength of his embrace.
His dark eyes, hypnotic in their mingled anger and
desire, held her as his lips demanded hers, demanded
her surrender and caused the growing fire within her
to unleash its force.

'That is a kiss,' she murmured after reading the first
five lines. She read further.
*His seeking mouth bruised her as she clung to him,
suddenly desperate for his love, wanting him as she had
wanted no other man. He had swept away all her anger,
her shame, and she was his.*
'Oo-oh, that's a kiss!' She leaned her head back, her
eyes rolling to the ceiling, just imagining Chuck kissing
her that way.
'I don't believe it.' He jerked the book out of her hand
and read the passage again.
'Well, don't worry about it.' Barbara tried to keep the
smugness of her ploy out of her voice. 'Nobody said you
had to be as good at making love as this guy. After all,
most women wouldn't know the difference.'
'I'm as good a lover as he is any day!' Chuck insisted as
his ego was punctured.
'If you say so.' Barbara let a little disbelief trail into
her voice, along with the dismissal she knew he wouldn't
accept.
'I am!'
She didn't answer, but let a half-smile curl her lips as
she took the book back, careful not to lose the place. She
let out a wistful sigh.

'Um-m-m—what a man!'

Chuck turned away, put his feet on the floor and reached forward to pick up his drink. From beneath her lashes she watched as he took a drink of the ouzo, and she had the satisfaction of seeing him shudder. But her ploy had not worked. According to her plan, he was supposed to prove what a good lover he was. It worked in chapter—she flipped the pages, careful to keep his place. Chapter Five, although Melissa had not intended the result of her remarks to Damon. Barbara skimmed their argument again, trying to figure out why it wasn't working for her.

Then suddenly the book was out of her hand, flying across the room, as Chuck grabbed her by the shoulder. His eyes were dark with determination.

'Come here, woman, and learn what a man *really* is,' he growled.

Barbara only had time to think his voice sounded more menacing than had the fictional hero's when she was summarily embraced. His lips came down on hers with all the bruising force the book had described. She wanted to fight him, to push him away. He was right, that wasn't what a woman really wanted. The anger of the display, the same that had been in the story, bruised more than her mouth, she felt used, taken. This wasn't the man she knew and loved.

Before she could free her arms, where they were imprisoned by his restricting embrace, he eased the pressure of his arms, but still held her as he looked into her startled and angry eyes.

'You can't tell me this isn't better.'

Before she could answer, his lips found hers again with a gentler, giving kiss carrying the warmth of banked fires, the deep repressed needs of a love that valued rather than possessed.

All Barbara's yearnings were brought out by the second lingering kiss. Her emotions swam in the sheltered bay of his arms as they held her. She felt protected, yet he had in his attitude left her the space to go to him, to move closer, to press forward with her own gift of need and the desire to please.

She eased the ache of her arms to hold him as they encircled his back, pulling him closer. Her pulses pounded as she returned the pressure of his lips on hers. This, she knew, was what she had been waiting for since she had first seen him. This was what all the books meant, but no author could fully express. She knew the reality of a world falling away—nothing existed but the two of them in that sea of desire that left them floating in each other's arms. Left nothing but the two of them in a world only they shared.

But it couldn't last, her logic warned her. Her body told her when Chuck came to the same conclusion. As realisation of what was happening to him, she felt first the drawing back of his emotion. When he pulled away, his breathing was slightly ragged. The surprised and confused look was back in his eyes, but he hid it quickly as he ran his hand through the sunbleached waves of his hair.

'Now don't tell me you didn't like that kiss,' he said, his voice hoarse but triumphant.

Barbara cocked her head to the side as if giving it some thought. She was stalling, trying to control her own rapid breathing and make her voice light. He had been shocked, she knew, and he must not be allowed to think about it too much. Her hopes would end in disaster if he thought she might be hurt by his romantic actions. She had to make him feel she only considered it an experiment.

'You do learn quickly,' she admitted. Her hand crept

down by her side, out of his sight. She crossed her fingers. She felt she needed that protection or the Guardians of Truth might shrivel her tongue for what she was about to say.

'It was a touch better than the other,' she said slowly. 'On a scale of ten, I would give it a four.'

Chuck's jaw dropped as he stared at her. 'A four? A *four*?' His indignation and anger was terrifying. She had felt a moment of doubt before she spoke, wondering if she would put a serious dent in his masculine pride. She certainly had. For a moment she wondered if he would hit her. She was relieved when he jumped to his feet and started pacing the room. Then he stopped and pointed an accusing finger at her.

'Ignorance,' he yelled at her. 'That's ignorance speaking. You don't know what a real kiss is.'

Over her fright, Barbara bounced back. 'Aren't we supposed to be learning?' she countered. 'When you learn, show me. I'd like to know.'

'Maybe I will and maybe I won't,' he said as he reached for his car keys. 'I'm not sure you'd appreciate it.

'Oh, but I would,' Barbara assured him. She wondered what else was wrong, the way he was staring down at his car keys. 'You don't have to go now, do you?'

'I might as well,' he muttered and turned towards the door. He was closing it behind him when he stopped and turned back. 'I'll tell you what *I'm* going to do.'

'What?' Barbara asked, hoping he wasn't so mad he'd fire her.

'*I'm* going to buy another book! That one's not doing what I want.'

Barbara smiled as she put the night latch on the door. In the kitchen, she washed the dishes and then prepared for bed. A few minutes later she was propped up against the pillows. The shaded lamp on the bedside stand cast a circle of light as she opened *Mediterranean Magic* and flipped the worn pages.

'Melissa,' she murmured. 'I think we'd better consider some alternatives.'

CHAPTER FIVE

THE next morning Barbara was taking her first sip of coffee when the doorbell chimed.

The cleaners? she thought, deciding they had started their deliveries early. She went to the bedroom and came back with her wallet, though the bell rang twice more before she opened the door. Instead of the boy with her delivery, Chuck stood in the hall.

'You don't need your wallet, I'll buy breakfast,' he said when he saw what she held in her left hand.

'Not for me you won't,' Barbara said as she closed the door behind him. 'This is Saturday, and I'm making waffles, bacon and eggs, and I'm doing it myself before I forget how to cook. I'm having a veritable orgy.'

Chuck grinned. 'Orgy? Can I play too?'

Not fully ready for the day, Barbara had no retort ready. She stepped into the cubicle that served as a kitchen in her flat, and brought out another cup of coffee. Chuck took it gratefully, drank part, then pulled a book from his back pocket and laid it on the table.

'That didn't help a bit,' he said, pointing to the glossy cover of the paperback. The title, *Sunset on Roses*, was unfamiliar to her.

Barbara picked it up and read the blurb on the back cover. 'No, I suppose the outback in Australia is a little far afield for us,' she said.

'I never thought of looking at the back,' Chuck admitted. 'And skip the cooking this morning, will you? Let's eat out. I don't want recipes and burning toast interrupting what I want to say.'

Barbara had planned her morning, and was looking forward to finishing her household tasks. She wanted the weekend free without the dread of laundry and dusting hanging over her head. But he seemed troubled. She sighed; her dream of accomplished chores fading in the land of unfulfilled hopes.

'The batter is made—I'll have to put it in the refrigerator,' Barbara said, getting up. Chuck followed her into the kitchen. On the counter sat a tray of bacon, still warm from the microwave oven. Barbara lifted the top of the waffle-iron, and took out a golden confection that made her regret for a moment that Chuck had shown up.

'On second thoughts, all you have to do is cook the eggs.' Chuck sniffed the aroma of bacon and eyed the waffle hungrily. 'I'll set the table.'

Breakfast was silent. They had known each other long enough to sit comfortably at the same table without talking, yet Barbara could tell by looking at Chuck that she was not shut out of his thoughts, and he certainly took a large place in hers.

When their appetites were sated, Barbara removed the plates and refilled their coffee cups. She waited until Chuck brought up the issue. He frowned slightly, thoughtfully.

'We're not going about this quite right. We're using a shot-gun technique on this problem, just blasting away.'

'You're saying we not aiming at a target?' Barbara asked.

'Right. We should know just what we're out to do. Then we can work towards it. Put it in words. Just what do *you* want?'

'Why me first?' Barbara objected. She was stalling, not knowing what to say.

'Well, we've got to start with someone, and it might as well be you.'

Yes, he would be concerned with what she wanted, that was like him, but Barbara couldn't tell him the truth. How did a woman look at a man across the breakfast table, a man she had known for over a year and a half and say 'I just want you?' If he had no idea after all that time, his shock would be devastating to her ego. His mind and heart were still loyal to Sandy. She was stuck with a nice, non-committal answer, one that would leave him comfortable, and again, give him no idea of her feelings.

She stirred her coffee, needlessly, since she drank it black.

'I guess I want what every woman wants. A home, a family, the picket fence and the station wagon. A man that loves me, needs me. Enough romance to keep the pulses going, enough trouble so I don't get jaded to the good things in life.'

'I thought you wanted the good life, the sophistication, the glamorous life,' Chuck said.

Barbara stirred her coffee again. Glamour was in a person's mind, she thought, and what could be better than what she had right now? She looked across at him, the overhead light making a halo of his freshly washed hair. His eyes, partly shaded because of the tilt of his head, were soft and concerned. She remembered his kiss the night before and thought nothing could ever thrill her as much, but she couldn't tell him that.

'If I have a choice, I'd like a little glitter—who wouldn't? I'm not going to sell myself for it—' She mustn't let him take that remark wrong, she thought. Sandy had money, but that was not the reason Chuck loved her, and Barbara didn't want to sound as if she thought he was attracted to the other woman because of her wealth. 'I mean, I'll take the glitter if it goes with love. I wouldn't just—' How did she get into such

confusing thoughts? She was babbling. She was trying to
tell him she'd take him any way he came, yet she couldn't
say it. She couldn't say she didn't want another man in
her life either. What a tangle.

'You want all you can get and still keep your integrity.'
His explanation, said as if it were a translation of her
tangled thoughts, was really a clarification of his own
position.

'And you?' She prompted him, wanting to turn the
subject away from herself. 'What do you want? Can you
put it in words?'

'I'm trying to zero in on it,' he answered.

'You want Sandy.' Barbara brought out the statement calmly. It was the first time she had been able to
say it outright. She was surprised she could do it so
calmly.

Chuck stared at his coffee for a moment, then looked
up and met her gaze. 'If I'm fortunate enough to win her,
I want to make her happy,' he said. 'The new fashion in
love is "Take me as you see me; if you love me, you'll
make the best of it." I think that's a cop-out. If I took
that attitude, it would be saying I didn't care enough
about her values to meet her half-way. That's love? If I
marry Sandy, I expect her to take some interest in the
things I care about. If I want a fair relationship, I'm
committed to do the same for her, right?'

Barbara nodded and stared out of the window, afraid
she was going to cry. Somewhere down inside her, she
had nourished a little hope that she was at least a little bit
wrong in her reading of Chuck's character. Lately, in
desperation, she had been hoping she would find a crack
in his sense of honour, a little more selfishness that
would prevent him from putting out the effort. But he
had dispelled that hope by putting into words what she
had believed of him. He really was as terrific as she had

thought, and Sandy was not the woman to recognise and appreciate him.

'And I guess I gave myself my own answer,' Chuck said.

'Uh, what—' Barbara had been so lost in her own thoughts she wasn't sure what he meant.

'I hadn't zeroed in,' he said patiently. 'I know what's important to me, but her desires are what I'm working for now—maybe not everything she wants, there's a limit to what anyone can give, but what I have to offer is hers by right.' He pointed a finger at her. 'And your answer will be the same. When you meet that great guy, then you'll know what to zero in on.'

There was just one fault in his reasoning, she decided. The guy she wanted, wanted Sandy, and she could never join him in that hope. She used the first objection that came to mind.

'But that's changing yourself, and changing me. We agreed in the beginning that to be phony wouldn't work.'

'It wouldn't work if it meant being phony,' he assured her. 'But two people with nothing in common aren't attracted to each other, unless it's purely physical. You're too smart to get caught in that trap. You won't lose your head over a hopeless case.'

Sez you, she thought. Aloud she said, 'So what does Sandy want? What does she most enjoy?'

Chuck sighed. 'She likes the country club. That's her set of friends, and she shares their interests. She goes in for golf, bridge, tennis. I don't think she'll ever get me to a bridge table, I don't like cards. My golf's okay, I took it in college.' He grinned, 'I needed a crash course. I haven't played tennis in years. I guess that's really the place I ought to start. Do you play?'

'I haven't played much since college,' Barbara said. 'But even if I did, I couldn't play at the country club.'

'Why not? They've got good courts, and members are allowed to bring guests.'

'Members don't bring their hired help,' Barbara retorted.

'You're not hired help!'

'Oh, who pays my salary?'

She had momentarily stopped him. His eyes flickered as he saw the sense in her answer, but he wasn't accepting it. Still, he didn't have a way around it, so he retorted in that classic manner of man overcoming female intelligence.

'Don't be stupid,' he demanded. 'Besides, I don't know anyone out there yet. If I went by myself, I'd just stand around looking foolish. I need you along to have someone to talk to—and who knows, you might meet your Damon.'

Yeah, get rid of me before Sandy gets back, Barbara thought. But he had spoken the magic words—he needed her. She admitted to herself that her capitulation was not entirely unselfish. If he started patronising the country club, she would be left out of his social life unless she went with him. She had a presentable tennis outfit and a good racket.

'If I have to change clothes, you wash the dishes,' she said, getting up from the table.

While Chuck rattled around in the kitchen, Barbara changed into the short white outfit and tied her hair back with a white silk scarf, working with it until, with the use of her hand-mirror, she was satisfied with the bow on the nape of her neck. When she re-entered the kitchen, Chuck was just putting away the plates.

'Ta-da-a-a!' Barbara sang herself some fanfare and struck a pose, but Chuck continued to fold and hang up the dish towel, keeping his back to her.

'Ready?' he asked, still not turning.

'Yeah,' the word dragged out. Nothing like falling on your ta-da-a-a to flatten the ego, Barbara thought.

But when he did notice her, his attention was all she could have asked. His look strayed appreciatively from the drawn-back hair down the shapely tennis outfit and caressed her long shapely legs. He gave a soft whistle.

'You can wear that to work anytime,' he said. 'On second thoughts, don't. I'd never get the drivers out on the road.'

Less than an hour later, they drove through the stone-pillared gates and up the winding drive of the country club. The old palms shaded the asphalt drive and the perfect lawn. Flowerbeds, their riotous colours contained by neat little hedges, dotted the grounds and bordered the old, sand-coloured, Spanish-style building.

Chuck parked the old jeep between a new Mercedes and a gleaming Porsche. He looked at the expensive cars and back at his own battered but beloved vehicle.

'I almost feel like covering it up with a blanket,' he said.

'You could drive a Mercedes if you wanted to,' Barbara came to his defence. Her loyal backing was unnecessary, she knew and so did he. She handled his bank deposits and knew his financial situation. There were few cars on the road that he could not buy outright that very day. Chuck drove his jeep because, like her with her Little Sadie, he was attached to it.

The Mexican influence on the outside of the building was carried throughout the lobby with its blue and white tiles, indoor fountain and heavy dark furniture, but Chuck didn't stop there. They dodged hanging pots of bright fuchsias as he led her down a hall to the right, coming out on a terrace flagged in earth-red tiles, interlaced with white grouting. The umbrellas of patio tables cast islands of shade over the ornate metal chairs.

They paused at the railing, flanked with earthenware pots of geraniums and marigolds. Below and accessible by a stairway were the tennis courts. Down on the green painted asphalt, the white lines vied with the clothing of the players for brilliance in the mid-morning sun.

All the courts were filled, but Barbara wasn't disappointed. The club was beautiful, and if they had to wait to play, she would not mind sitting, surrounded by bright flowers, enjoying the laughter and light conversation coming from the courts and the few occupants of the terrace.

Chuck pulled out a chair from one on the shaded tables, and when she was seated, he laid his racket beside hers. With his customary determination, he strolled off down the terrace to get a better view of the other courts.

Barbara watched him go. Reluctantly, she admitted that away from her, he changed in her eyes. Divorced from all visible touch with the trucking company, he seemed to belong on that terrace. As he walked along, looking over the courts, he was the personification of his surroundings.

His well-fitting white shorts and knitted shirt with the green and yellow trim was the uniform of a club where people negotiated a thin line between their individuality and the conformity required for togetherness. Physically he far surpassed most of the men Barbara could see on the courts. By their puffing and paunches, a few were out for the exercise, rather than the game itself. Others appeared in good physical condition and were excellent players, but Chuck, walking slowly between the tables, could have been the model for all of them, Barbara thought.

The sunlight, falling on him as he stepped between the tables, caused the light hair on his legs and arms to flash gold in the sunlight. As he reached the end of the terrace and started back, he changed his course slightly, and encountered a pot of geraniums that blocked his path. His effortless leap as he cleared the plant and continued on his way was poetry of energy in action, Barbara thought.

As he approached the table, Barbara pulled her thoughts in order.

'We've hit another check,' she said.

'Maybe we should sign up for a court,' Chuck said. 'I'll see.'

But while he was speaking, the couple on the nearer court hailed them. The man came their way.

'Interested in doubles?' he called through the wire fence. 'Our opposition didn't show up.'

'That depends.' Chuck's answer surprised Barbara. 'Were they intimidated by your skill?'

The man laughed. 'They didn't want to be embarrassed, playing with duffers like us.'

Barbara and Chuck walked to the gate in the protective wire fence and entered the enclosure as the other couple came forward to meet them. She and Chuck shook hands with Marie and Jim Dennis. Marie was about five feet six inches tall and slim; Barbara thought they probably wore the same size in clothes. Jim was nearly six feet, and like Marie had dark hair and dark blue eyes. Jim was well built and muscular. Barbara doubted either he or Marie were duffers on the tennis court.

'Don't get time to play as much as I'd like,' Jim was telling Chuck, though Barbara could feel his eyes on her as she took the cover off her racket. Feeling out of place in the surroundings, she couldn't help wondering if he had seen her somewhere and wondered what she was doing in the exalted company of the country club.

She was a little nervous when she took her place on the court and waited for the first serve, but once the ball was in action, she forgot her worries. She was delighted to be in the game again.

She was surprised at her own play and Chuck's. Her tennis racket had been gathering dust for several years, but she could have been slamming balls around only the day before. She had never heard Chuck mention tennis, and doubted that he had played in the past several years, but he was all over the court; his returns were hard-driven and sure. Barbara was in awe of his back-hand.

As she suspected, the Dennises weren't novices at the game, and they took the first game, forty-thirty, but the set went to Chuck and Barbara. Two more games and by mutual agreement they gave over the court to another foursome while they took a break.

They took a seat at one of the tables, and Jim signalled for a waiter. Barbara laughed as Marie chided her partner for one of his serves and he cheerfully accused her of wearing lead boots. Barbara admired their relationship, thinking they must have a good marriage until Marie leaned over to speak to Chuck, attempting to enlist him on her side of the argument. The smile Jim gave Barbara was not that of a loving husband. It clearly said, 'I'd like to get to know you better.' Repelled, she moved slightly, and turned to join in the conversation between Marie and Chuck.

If Barbara had any doubts about the meaning of Jim's smile, a young woman just coming out onto the terrace dispelled them for her. The look she gave the dark-haired man left no room for conjecture. Dead romances had a certain unmistakable air. Barbara could admire his taste, the girl was lovely, but she had no use for a character who obviously felt no responsibility for the gold band on Marie's finger.

The waiter arrived and after a hurried discussion, they settled on fresh lemonade. Then Jim tapped Marie on the arm.

'What time is Frank expecting you home?' he asked and grinned at Barbara. 'My brother is very protective of his wife.'

'I must have forgotten to tell you—he's going to be out of town till Tuesday,' Marie answered with the hollow tone of a falsity. Barbara had seen the surprised look on Marie's face change to understanding, and a knowledgeable smile. She turned back to Chuck, who had just knocked over his tennis racket. He was twisted around in his chair as he picked it up and missed the interplay of looks.

Barbara tried to look upon Jim with a kinder eye. His smile had been offensive to her only because she thought he was a married man. And he had been embarrassingly obvious about letting her know he wasn't, but he had certainly cleared up the misunderstanding. She didn't care for men who tried to move in on women they had just met, but then some people formed relationships on the spur of the moment. But how did he know she and Chuck weren't romantically involved, even though she didn't wear a ring? Perhaps he was testing the water, trying to find out.

Chuck, knowing nothing of the silent communications, turned the conversation back to tennis and its famous players. Barbara sat back and listened, marvelling that she had known him for over a year and a half, and had no idea he was so interested in sport, or that he kept up with the tournaments. Jim did his part, talking easily about the famous matches he had seen.

'You were there,' Chuck commented as Jim related a

story of an encounter between two players that did not take place on the courts.

'Occasionally I get to a match,' Jim said easily. 'I'm a nut over the sport, but I spend more time watching than I do playing. Business usually keeps me off the courts.'

Barbara drank her lemonade, leaned back and listened to the conversation of the three others. The talk drifted into business, and Marie joined the conversation. Her comments showed she took an active interest in the advertising company run by her husband and her brother-in-law.

Left out of the conversation by her own choice, Barbara let her mind go for a general absorption of the scene. She decided she too could grow used to the graces of attractive surroundings. Usually her Saturday mornings were devoted to cleaning her flat and doing the laundry. Playing tennis and sitting on a terrace drinking lemonade was a welcome change. But what she liked most was the change she saw in Chuck. The night before, he had been wire-tight, out to prove something. Today, in the company of Jim and Marie, he was at ease, enjoying himself.

Those social graces they were trying to develop were his naturally. He was intelligent and articulate, a man who thought, and could, by a simple question or observation, turn a conversation from merely polite to absorbingly interesting. As important, his ingrained courtesy assured his listener of his undivided attention, a form of flattery to which no one was immune.

And he *looked* as if he belonged, Barbara thought as she watched him suddenly lean back in his chair, his eyes raised to the inner lining of the canvas umbrella that covered the table. His sensuous lips were slightly parted, his tongue appeared in the corner of his mouth as he thought over something Jim said. Barbara had missed it.

Then Chuck leaned forward again, picking up his half-empty glass and tilting it slightly as he used it for emphasis for his answer.

Yes, she decided, he was stepping into a world where he fitted, where he would be right at home, because being a giver, he had something to offer that would overshadow any smallness of attitude of those around him. He didn't need that sophistication he was trying to develop.

So where did that leave her? Barbara wondered. Nowhere, she decided. His problems with Sandy had been his lack of interest in a social life, but a year before he had been suffering from too many business pressures for lighter activities to have a place in his mind. Now he was freer, and he had certainly shown he could get along with the people in Sandy's world. Barbara sighed, thinking she could be wrong, perhaps he would be happier with Sandy. But somehow she could not accept that.

'That okay with you?' Chuck asked her.

'Uh—what?' Barbara looked at him blankly. She had not heard a word of the conversation at the table.

'To come back tonight for dinner and dancing,' Chuck said.

Marie smiled across the table. 'We'll make a party of it. Jim's instructed by his brother to see to it that I don't sit at home and mope.'

'He's senior partner, so I have to take orders,' Jim laughed. His eyes travelled to Barbara again. His expression was significant, but she was unable to read his meaning. Still, his gaze had called for an answer. If she snubbed him, she and Chuck would be alone that evening, even if they did come to the club. Since Chuck wanted to get to know a few members so he would feel at home, she could not throw cold water on his chance to start circulating. Though he had not expressed it, his ego demanded that if this was Sandy's world, he wanted to show her he could make a go of it without her backing and introductions. Barbara could not thwart that desire, it would be cheating. She gave Jim a smile in return, hoping it appeared as non-committal as she meant it to be.

They made plans to meet again at eight o'clock and departed. The rest of the day's activities became complicated and convoluted. With the afternoon free, Chuck decided to give Little Sadie a check-over to see what was causing the missing. That entailed returning to her flat so she could drive the Volkswagen back to the office. Since she had a few personal errands to run, she took Chuck's jeep. When she finished her shopping and went back to the company again, Little Sadie's parts were spread out all over the workshop.

'You're without a car for the rest of the weekend,' Chuck told her when he picked her up.

'You broke it,' Barbara accused.

'I think it tried to commit suicide—but don't worry, a rebuilt carburetor and you'll be back on the road. I can't get one until Monday.'

Barbara chaffed at the expense, but consoled herself by deciding the occasional part she had to buy was far easier on her wallet than monthly payments.

At home again she rushed around to finish her chores. She wanted to allot some time to pampering herself before they went back to the club. Nothing made a woman feel more gorgeous than a long, hot, luxurious bath, attention to all the small details of meticulous grooming and giving herself a manicure.

By seven o'clock she was dressed, wearing a teal blue silk dress with a wide neckline, cap sleeves and a full, gored skirt. She moved away from her full-length mirror, watching over her shoulder as the delicate silk swayed

and floated on the air currents. It seemed to say a
disturbing presence has passed, take notice. She smiled
and nodded, liking the effect, hoping it would bring out
some reaction in the only person she was interested in
impressing.

As a final touch she fastened the catch of a pearl
necklace that her father had given her when she gradu-
ated from Business College. The lustre of the pearls
glowed against her skin and the dress caused her eyes to
look a deeper blue. She admired the result with the
casual curls, pinned up on her head, and the wisps that
hinted nonchalance behind the careful arrangement.

When the doorbell rang at five minutes after seven,
she was ready. Chuck was not due for another twenty-
five minutes, but being early was his main flaw and she
had learned to live with it.

When she opened the door, Barbara clamped her lips
shut to keep from saying something foolish. She had had
a day of learning about Chuck, but apparently he still
had some surprises left to spring. In a tailored dinner-
jacket and black tie, he was a knockout. The white
brought out his golden tan and set off the blonde in his
sunbleached brown hair. But the tennis outfit had done
that. Barbara decided it was the elegance of his clothes,
and the way he wore them. No one would ever believe he
spent many of his days in a denim work shirt with grease
on one sleeve. She felt as if he were suddenly some
stranger, truly the hero of a novel instead of familiar and
comfortable Chuck. Her hesitation was mirrored in his
face.

'Are you sure you didn't step out of a magazine?' he
asked slowly as he stepped in and closed the door. 'You
could be on the cover of—' Apparently his imagination
had not stretched far enough for a name, but his meaning was clear. Clear, too, was the way he looked at her.

She knew he approved of what he saw, yet she wasn't the Barbara he knew, and like her, he was counting on a supporting familiarity in a new situation. But he recovered quickly.

'Well, we ought to knock them dead,' he said lightly. 'Men wear the standard uniform, so it's left to the woman on his arm to make a guy look good. I should be the envy of every man there.'

'I'll try to do you justice,' Barbara said as she led the way into the living-room. Then, unable to resist it, she turned to gaze at him again. 'That's not going to be easy.' Then she noticed the drops of water on his hair. 'Is it raining?'

'Off and on.'

Barbara was surprised. She had been so busy with her preparations she hadn't noticed, but as she listened through the open window she could hear the swish of cars running on wet roads. Her practical side saw disaster for their evening.

'How are we going to get to the club? Little Sadie is out of action, and we can't ride in an open jeep.'

'Leave it to the master,' Chuck grinned. 'Let's go, woman. Big doin's in the works.'

As Chuck held the street door for her, Barbara opened her umbrella and looked about as he stepped beneath the shelter with her. They were out on the pavement and walking along past a number of parked cars when Chuck caught her arm and stopped her.

'Your carriage, Cinderella.'

Barbara stared. She stood looking at a gleaming Mercedes.

'What—'

Chuck grinned. 'Cinderella needed a coach.'

'But where did you get it?' Barbara kept staring at the car as if it really was a transformed pumpkin. When

Chuck opened the door she slid in on the leather interior and waited for him to come around the car and get in under the wheel.

'Remember Mr Gresham?' Chuck asked as he fumbled to find the ignition.

Barbara nodded. She remembered the old gentleman who called occasionally and expected Chuck to drop everything to handle some handyman or mechanic chore for him. He had been one of Chuck's odd-job customers when he worked his way through college, and the old man never seemed to understand that phase of Chuck's life was over. Mainly, Barbara thought, because Chuck never insisted.

'You borrowed it,' she said, referring to the car.

'Nope,' Chuck cautiously manoeuvered out of the parking place, double checking before he changed gear and generally exploring the newness of command. 'He's retiring—it's about time, he's eighty-six—going to Florida to live with his daughter. He wanted me to look it over and tune it so he could sell it. I don't know how he can foul up an engine like he does. But this time he had help. He let one of his great-nephews work on it.'

'It's that five-mile-an-hour driving,' Barbara just repeated what she'd heard Chuck complain of.

'Yea, anyway, what's the point in my tuning it up for someone else, when I need a car anyway? There's too much going on—I don't have time to go car shopping. I mean it fell in my lap—and I have to do the work anyway—and since it was me, he let me have it at a good price—'

Chuck was using his hands to explain. Barbara knew he was making excuses, not for her as much as for himself. He had bought it, but he had wanted a new car. Now he was trying to talk himself into being satisfied. He had visualised himself going in and buying a car from a showroom, she guessed. That would have been in keeping with his new image. He wasn't quite satisfied that his bargain came to him as a result of his grease-monkey days.

'I'm so glad you got it,' Barbara said. 'At least you know this one. It won't be a stranger—you've tuned it up before, you know all its idiosyncrasies.'

Babble to make him feel good. Even Barbara knew old Mr Gresham had bought a new car only months ago. It was this year's model and had not yet been in Chuck's hands for a tune-up—and it certainly needed one. It chugged and sputtered worse than Little Sadie. But that was a minor detail. Chuck was a whiz with cars, especially diesels.

'Oh, I've got to stop at the shop,' Chuck announced as he turned the corner.

'You're not going to work in your dinner-jacket, and besides the Dennises are expecting us.'

'I'm not going to work,' Chuck agreed. 'I think I forgot to lock up the shop. I just want to check.'

'Okay, but no work,' Barbara cautioned. Part of her concern was for herself. Without a helper, he might enlist her to hand him tools. It had happened before.

Chuck was wrong. He had not forgotten to lock the shop. He even checked Little Sadie. She was also locked up tight. Only one thing was missing.

'Where's the jeep?' Barbara asked as he got back into the car and shut the door.

'I lent it to Otis. He'll bring it back Monday morning,' Chuck said as he put the key in the ignition again. He gave Barbara a grin. 'Well, here we go—off to the ball.'

The Mercedes didn't start.

CHAPTER SIX

'WHAT'S the matter?' Barbara asked as Chuck leaned back in the seat, his eyes closed. His frustration filled the air in the car until she could hardly breathe.

'I don't know.' Chuck sighed and struck the steering-wheel with the palms of his hands, temporarily defeated. 'Gresham let his great-nephew work on it, I think. I wouldn't hazard a guess until I've checked half a dozen things.'

'You can't do that tonight.' On the way home from the club that afternoon, he had been full of talk about the people who were supposed to be fellow guests of the Dennises for dinner. He wanted to meet a few people other than Sandy's intimate group before she returned. Not that he wanted to show off, but he needed, for his own self-respect, to know he could live in her world without her help. He could not arrive late at the club, covered with grease.

'No, not tonight, but I wish I hadn't taken the carburettor out of the Volks.'

'Oh.' Barbara caught the implication. He'd lent out the jeep, too. They were temporarily out of vehicles. But Chuck wasn't to be stopped. They went into the office where she checked the telephone directory for taxis, and he telephoned. The rain and other pressures were tying up the cabs. Barbara was becoming increasingly discouraged with every call and his voice grew more irritated after each request and refusal. Then Chuck tapped the thick directory.

'Check limousines.'

'Limousines?' Barbara repeated incredulously. She couldn't believe what she was hearing. He was really going first-class. He took her surprise to be a joke, as if she were feigning it. His eyes went grey with irritation. He checked his watch for the fourth time in fifteen minutes.

'We want to get there, don't we?'

Barbara found the listings. They numbered more than twenty. Ten didn't answer. Seven had recorded messages. One was a horse and carriage. The others were booked solid.

Barbara sat in her secretary's chair while Chuck lounged on the corner of the desk. They stared out into the gathering darkness, wondering what to do.

Shame, she thought, that the four perfectly running vehicles sitting in the yard were all the big diesel cabs, two at the moment detached from their trailers. Chuck picked up her mental comment so quickly, it could have been spoken.

His gaze lingered first on the newest of the trucks, and then fell to meet hers. His look had its own shrug, it could have been physical.

'Excuse me for thinking about it,' is what she read in his eyes.

'I shouldn't forgive you for even considering driving one tonight,' her blue glance spoke quickly and decisively. She stared through the window for a moment and then back at him. Her 'I won't do it, so don't ask me,' was not oral. Her attention kept returning to the big diesels.

He, too, was looking back and forth between the cabs and Barbara. His 'I'm out of ideas,' was not quite a plea; it was a statement, inviting any suggestions.

Her capitulation took in more than her eyes, her whole face said, 'Okay, but the things I go through for you shouldn't happen to your worst enemy.'

Barbara followed as Chuck led the way out to the cab of the big semi. She forced her feet. They assumed the weight of reluctance, but she made them follow. She waited while Chuck unlocked the door on the passenger's side and stood frozen as the enormity of what they were doing struck her.

Enormity was the word for it. She stared up at the big GM vehicle. At that moment it was her personal Mount Everest. In the year and a half she had worked for Chuck she had never been so forcibly struck by the size of the diesel cabs. Maybe, she thought, that was because she had never thought of climbing in one dressed for a dance. She stared at the huge front wheel, waist high on her, and the floor-board was at eye level. Above it was the door and the seat she was to occupy. To reach it, she had to climb the welded foot holds and the chrome ladder and then swing to the right to get into the cab.

She was thankful the rain had stopped, but the side of the truck, the small metal steps and the chrome ladder all sparkled with drops of water.

'I'll never make it in these clothes,' she muttered. She shook her head and tentatively reached for the chrome bar that gleamed wetly from the intermittent showers. Her full, flowing silk skirt came perilously close to the tyre. She stepped back.

'I'll ruin my dress!' She was half angry with Chuck for lending the Jeep, for taking the carburettor out of Sadie, and for putting her in such a ridiculous position.

'Well—hold your skirt back with one hand.'

'Are you crazy? Not even you can climb in that thing one-handed—not with rain on the ladder rungs, and in slick shoes.' Her anger was moving past the half mark and aiming for full.

'Sure I could,' he sounded hesitant. She could tell by his tone he wasn't bragging. His argument was only to cover his disappointment. His lips pursed as he mentally searched for an answer. Her sympathy for him left no room for anger.

'I honestly don't think I can do it,' she warned him, 'but just let me get in the mood. Ooh-hoo-hoo— she mimicked a chimpanzee, rapidly scratching at her shoulder and thigh. 'You've got to be half ape, I think.'

Her change of attitude brought a grin from Chuck. 'Yeah, that's it. Now you hold your skirt with one hand and I'll balance you.'

Barbara took a deep breath and managed the two welded steel steps. Her right foot was groping for the chrome ladder on the side of the cab when she started to swing off balance. Chuck made a grab to catch her.

'Watch what you're pushing!' she demanded and jumped to the ground.

'You wiggled while I was reaching,' Chuck defended himself. 'Here, let's try something else. Forget the ladder. Take your skirt in your left hand—now hold the bar with your right and step up on the first step—'

'This isn't going to work,' Barbara complained. The big bar he was speaking of had to be on her left when she climbed in. Nevertheless, she did as he instructed.

'That's right,' He stepped close, his hand on the bar just under hers. 'Now just sit back.'

At that moment his idea sounded like the only solution. Barbara gingerly allowed her weight to rest on his shoulder.

'Let the bar go,' Chuck said. He removed his hand before she gathered her nerve to break away from her only stable support. That was their undoing. Chuck, already beginning to move and leaning against the resistance of her hand on the support bar, staggered. Barbara, sitting on his shoulder, was helpless as he swayed. She let out a squeal as he staggered. She felt as if she were in a small boat on a storm-tossed ocean. When he regained his balance they were six feet from the truck and facing in the opposite direction. For a moment they were both too breathless to speak.

'Are you giving me a ride to the country club?' Barbara asked.

'Any more smart remarks and I'll drop you,' Chuck warned. He carefully moved back to the truck.

'Now put your feet on the tires—no! Don't stick those spike heels in the tire!'

'I want to go home!' Barbara wailed as she stood on the tire, her hands welded to the chrome handles by her fear, afraid to raise one foot to the carpeting of the truck's floor-board.

'If you go home, you get out by yourself,' Chuck panted. 'Now, let's get this circus act on the road. Are you going to get in, or am I going to push?'

'You beast,' Barbara said as she gathered her courage and took the final step. Inside she settled herself on the seat and glared down at him as he closed the door.

'What a place to spend the rest of my life,' she muttered, looking around at the interior of the truck. She knew she'd never have the nerve to get out.

'Here we go,' Chuck said as he climbed in and put the key in the ignition. Across the wide expanse of the 'dog house', he seemed miles away. The leather upholstered box that separated the driver from the passenger covered part of the engine that would take them to the country club, but at the moment Barbara resented it. She felt the need for close companionship, and it kept her so far away from Chuck.

But once the wail and roar of starting the diesel engine had died to a muted thunder, and they were on their way, Barbara felt the elation known only to the men called 'Knights of the Road'. All the frustrations of climbing into the truck were forgotten as she looked down on the tops of the parked cars. When a Volkswagen, pulling out from a side street, caused Chuck to slow the truck, Barbara felt as if she could reach out and flick the tiny thing away. How dare it impede the progress of their magnificent monster?

The idea brought out a self-conscious giggle.

'What's funny?' Chuck asked and Barbara told him. To her it was silly, and while she trusted him not to laugh at her, she was surprised to see the naked approval in his eyes.

'You just took your first test as driver, but I'm not sure you passed,' he replied.

'What do you mean by that crack?' Barbara was half offended.

'That's the one thing a truck driver has to guard against. It's the God complex. Up here you tend to get the feeling you're a superior being. You have to be careful. It's hard to remember when you're looking down on them, that those insignificant little vehicles have a right to use *your* road too.'

From her position, Barbara could well understand that. She had never suspected that an elevated position could so elevate the ego. She flipped her hand as if the other people were nothing.

'Just run them down. How dare they use *our* road?'

'Let's see how you like some of our other roads,' Chuck laughed as he pulled onto the entrance ramp of the freeway. On the city streets the ride had been smooth, but the accelerated speeds of the major highway caused her to feel she was sitting in a milkshake machine.

Beneath her, the huge engine seemed to be straining to break away from Chuck's control. Like a restive horse, it lunged, paused to gather its strength, tried a couple of tentative leaps and plunged forward again.

'Is—it—it—alwa-al-always—?' she tried to question Chuck, but he just laughed.

After they had travelled a couple of miles, she noticed a rhythm to the movement of the truck.

'Would it be smo-smoother if we were pulling a load?' she shouted over the noise of the engine and the rattling.

'It's not the truck, it's the concrete road. Not much difference if we were pulling a trailer.'

Barbara settled back, keeping her feet braced. She kept a wary eye on her handbag as it bounced about on the top of the dog house. Like riding a vibrator with the hiccups, she thought.

She had a few minutes to catch her breath when they left the freeway and drove the few blocks to the country club. She had ceased to worry about how she was going to get out of the truck, but when they turned into the pillar-flanked entrance to the club, the problem came back again with a slam. Even Chuck was worried.

'I didn't expect this,' he said as they stopped behind a line of cars waiting for valet parking. As they watched one car pulled up to the canopied entrance, the occupants stepped out and a young man in a jacket drove the Cadillac away.

'Big hitch in our plans,' Chuck muttered. 'Those kids could never drive this thing, much less park it. They'd squash a Mercedes and two Porsches, just trying to back this baby.'

'And don't you dare let them try!' Half incensed, half terrified, Barbara was nearly screaming. After the fiasco of getting into the truck, she was getting out *sans* audience or setting up housekeeping right where she was.

Chuck nodded and pulled out of the line. He seemed to understand her need for the darkest, most private part of the parking lot in which to make her descent, and parked the truck where the palms gave a camouflaging shade and the bulk of the huge diesel tractor would hide her from the club's arrivals.

When he opened her door, he had a plan she could hardly fault.

Carefully instructing her so she held on to the climbing bars, he guided her feet until she was securely standing on the big tire. Then as she leaned forwards his strong arms came up. Catching her around the waist, he gently lifted her out. She caught her breath as she was imprisoned in his embrace. The safety, the security his strong arms communicated was for a moment lost in the thrill of being so close to him. All the frustrations were left behind as she looked up at him.

Chuck, too, seemed loath to break the embrace. He gazed into her eyes, his own seeming to ask questions that required answers from within. Barbara held her breath, hoping, praying the solutions he found would be in her favour. But he turned the moment's mood with a question.

'Find the ground okay? Feel comfortable again?'

Barbara nodded, not quite trusting her voice. She wanted to demand an answer to those enigmatic expressions in his eyes, but the fear that she might come out to be the loser kept her quiet. The shower, so light it was more a falling mist, had started again, and they walked across the parking lot sheltered under Barbara's umbrella. Out of the corner of her eye she saw Chuck glancing at the cars they passed. She felt his pain. He had wanted to drive up to the door that night in a vehicle he could be proud of. Instead, he had been forced to park the GM tractor back in the shadows. Barbara wanted desperately to ease that disappointment.

'Insignificant little creatures, these Porsches and

Jaguars. And I bet no two of them could match the investment of *our* chariot.'

Chuck, lost in his disappointment, was a moment taking in the full meaning of her remark. She was rewarded with his dawning understanding, the lightening of his eyes, and an effervescence of gratitude that bubbled up and exploded into words and action.

'You really are *something else*!' Whirling around, he grabbed her in his arms. Unmindful of the rain, he kissed her, his lips warm on hers, his arms sheltering her from the world as he communicated his appreciation, the sharing of his happiness.

Barbara tried to force her mind to quiet, reminding herself there was nothing loverlike in his embrace, but her heart read into it all the wonders of love desired and received. The forgotten umbrella fell from her hand as her arms went around him, returning all the longings she tried to keep hidden.

The blast of a horn and a good-natured laugh recalled them to their surroundings.

'Hey, we're not only getting wet, we're holding up traffic.' Chuck laughed as he stepped away from her and rescued the umbrella that was rolling between two waiting cars in line for parking.

Barbara stood a little breathless. True, his kiss had not been that of a lover, but it had been spontaneous and full of affection. She walked at his side through the heavy mist and thought the light rain was as beautiful as starlight, as moonlight on the Mediterranean.

As they strolled across the lobby, Marie came out of the cocktail lounge. When she saw Barbara and Chuck, she waved gaily.

'I'm glad you made it. Such a tangle of traffic out there—it's just a little rain, but you'd think it was a foot of snow.'

'We're a little late.' In stating the obvious, Chuck was apologising without being servile about it.

'We were too, and the others haven't made it yet,' Marie turned her attention to Barbara, her beautifully shaped eyebrows went up as her mouth formed an oval. 'I *like* that dress! Come with me to the powder room and let's repair the ravages of the weather. Rain can be so inconsiderate.'

While Chuck headed for the bar, Barbara followed Marie into the ladies' lounge. They sat on the delicate chairs facing the wall-size mirror behind a long, ornate make-up table. While Barbara tucked in an obstinate curl, Marie freshened her lipstick. Barbara's lighter complexion called for a paler gloss that had not shown wear.

When Marie closed her handbag, she turned a thoughtful gaze on Barbara. 'I keep feeling I've seen Chuck before—I can't remember where—' Her eyes flickered as if she might have stepped into forbidden territory. She smiled and waved the question away. 'Probably at traffic lights. I have the craziest memory—I never forget a face, but never remember where I saw it.'

Barbara could have let the comment pass, but sooner or later the truth would emerge, and until it did, she would feel like a usurper, being accepted on false pretences. Chuck had not suggested she keep her identity a secret, and she saw no reason to do so.

'You probably saw him here at the club,' she said casually. 'He's been dating Sandy Harrington.'

'Oh,' Marie tried to find a place to anchor her self-conscious look, anywhere but on Barbara's face. She opened her handbag again.

'Yes, Sandy's responsible for Chuck being a member,' Barbara went on. 'While she's out of town, I'm pinch-hitting. I'm his secretary/Girl Friday.'

Her explanation eased Marie's discomfort. Barbara was gratified to notice the admission that she was not born with the proverbial silver spoon had not brought out disapproval in Marie. The brunette brightened. 'Then it's not—uh—you and Chuck are not—'

'No romance,' Barbara finished for her. No romance. Half the truth; it did take two, after all.

Marie looked as if she wanted to say something she shouldn't. Barbara waited, not sure whether to prompt her or not. Finally her curiosity got the better of her discretion.

'You look as if you're about to say something naughty. I'm dying to hear it.'

'Well,' Marie glanced around, the classic gesture preceding a confidence. 'If you think anything of him, steer someone else into his life. Sandy Harrington is—' she paused, settling for a considered description, '—not the world's best choice for the boss's wife. I knew her at school.'

Barbara nodded. 'Not that I'll have much to say in the choosing,' she said, but she *was* relieved. At times she had wondered if she was distorting Sandy by viewing her with jealous eyes. Marie's opinion added weight to her determination to save Chuck from Sandy.

'We'd better get back,' Marie said as she stood up and checked her skirt for wrinkles. 'The birthday girl should be around for her own party, I suppose.'

'Oh,' Barbara smiled. 'Happy birthday!'

Marie arched her brows again as she flipped her skirt playfully. 'The present I expect to be given is silence on the question of which one.' She led the way back to the lounge.

Chuck and Jim were sitting with another couple. Barbara was introduced to Pete and Verna Rose. They were both in their mid-sixties, with the bright eyes and glowing skin of people who devoted themselves to physical exercise. Marie explained the relationship. Pete was her maternal uncle, and until his retirement, he had been the attorney for the Dennis Advertising firm.

'And I'm probably the only one here who knows just which birthday you're celebrating,' Pete said to Marie.

'You just keep that information to yourself.' Marie gave him a playful slap on the arm.

Marie and Pete bickered cheerfully as they led the way to the dining-room. Jim took Barbara's arm, and Chuck and Verna followed.

On the way across the lobby, Barbara felt the weight of a strange gaze. She looked up just in time to catch the jealous stare of a tall, willowy redhead. Another conquest Jim had left behind, she thought. But it was none of her business. She turned her attention back to the teasing between Marie and Pete.

'They sound like age-old enemies,' Jim said to Barbara with a smile.

'Watch the remarks on age,' Marie quipped.

Chuck and Verna were laughing at the argument, but Barbara was beginning to feel slightly uncomfortable. Jim kept smiling at her; his eyes held an invitation to get better acquainted. With not the slightest interest in him, Barbara was at a loss to know how to react. To encourage him would build a situation she would rather avoid, but she could hardly snub him. She was glad when they reached the table and were busy with the menus.

The dining-room was only partially filled when they entered. As in all large, partially empty rooms, the occupants were slightly subdued, as if no one wanted to be the one to break the hush. The conversations were soft, like the spills of candle-light that flowed from the flower-circled glass globes on the table. The sparkle of silver and crystal, the soft light on the faces cast a romantic spell around the room.

Dinner was excellent. Only the conversation left something to be desired. Barbara could sympathise with the four old friends. The Roses had just returned from Europe and were full of stories about their mutual friends. Good manners demanded they include Chuck and Barbara in the talk about the table, and she could see their efforts to keep the conversation general. Still, every few minutes the desire to impart some gossip from abroad was irresistible.

They were like children, trying to wait for Christmas dinner, yet unable to resist sampling the icing on the cake.

To Barbara's surprise it was Chuck who freed them of their guilt and let them talk. Once when Pete slipped into a story and was struggling for a way to get out of it, Chuck spoke up abruptly.

'But their daughter, the sculptress,' he said, referring back to a conversation earlier in the evening. 'Did she go on to Belgium after all?'

'Now, that's the funny part—' Pete half turned to Chuck, his face alight with his tale. 'After raising all that fuss—'

Barbara sat listening and paid closer attention to Chuck's occasional remarks. She wondered how he remembered the strange names and incidents from which he formed his comments and questions. He did it so smoothly; was it an acquired talent or the instinct of his generous nature?

Chuck seemed to be having such a good time, she thought it a shame that he spent so much time working over his business. He had a need for people, a need to laugh that she had not until now recognised. She wondered again if she was wrong when she hoped to best

Sandy and win Chuck for herself. Could she be doing him a disservice?

Before she had time to think about it the musicians took their place on the bandstand, and Pete was on his feet, asking Verna to dance. Chuck was not long delayed in leading her on the floor as the band played an old favourite.

'How do you like the party?' Chuck asked as he led her around the floor.

'Marvellous, they're a lot of fun,' Barbara murmured. She didn't dare add her true opinion. Much as she had enjoyed the banter around the table, she wished they could stay on the dance floor for the rest of the evening. Chuck's arms around her kept her breathless with delight. They moved together so well, they seemed to fit together as if fate had moulded them for each other.

She raised her eyes to his as he looked down, a soft smile played on his lips, his eyes were slightly dreamy with the music, the wine and the evening. His gaze encompassed her in his enjoyment, she was a part of it. At that moment he was not thinking of Sandy, she could tell. As he applied a slight pressure she moved closer, fitting close against him, feeling the movement of his body as he communicated the movement of the dance. Her sigh was soft, quiet, forcibly held in check. To let him know how her blood raced at their closeness, at how the touch of his body caused her to yearn for more of him would ruin everything. Like all beautiful moments the dance seemed to end too soon.

During the evening she danced three times with Chuck. Her two excursions on to the floor with Jim left her uncomfortable. He was too attentive. She had been concerned that he would be a snuggler, but apparently he was too polished in his style to be publicly embarrassing. Instead, his charm, not completely feigned, seemed to search for cracks in her emotional armour.

After her third dance with Chuck, they reached the table to find Pete and Jim back in their chairs, but Marie and Verna had stopped at another table to chat. Chuck was pulling out Barbara's chair when Pete stood up.

'May I borrow Barbara for a dance?' he asked Chuck. 'I can't resist a rumba.'

Barbara found herself back out on the floor again. The Latin dance was stimulating, and she enjoyed it. Pete was a good dancer, and his jokes kept her laughing. She was still flushed with pleasure when they arrived back at the table, but her enjoyment suffered a setback. Before she was settled in her chair, she could tell something was bothering Chuck. To the others she was sure he seemed the same, but his attitude was lacking an almost indefinable sparkle, recognisable only to someone who knew him very well. A few minutes later they made their excuses and left the club.

'Oh, oh,' she said as they crossed the parking lot and approached the truck. 'I forgot I still have to climb Mount Everest.'

'Shall I climb in and pull, or stay behind and push?' Chuck asked, grinning.

'Turn your back.'

'What?'

'Do as I say!' Barbara was slightly exasperated. She knew how to get in by herself, but she had to be without an audience. While they were arguing, someone else might come out of the club. But with a shrug, Chuck obeyed.

During the evening, Barbara had remembered the 'prom climb,' as they called it when she was a teenager. They had used it for last-minute decorating repairs when already in their long dresses. She caught up the back of her skirt, brought it up between her legs and tucked it in her belt. She looked as if she were playing the part of the King of Siam. Not too romantic but it did the job. Hurriedly she climbed up the ladder, swung into the cab and had freed her skirt by the time Chuck turned.

'How did you do that?' He looked outraged. She could hardly blame him after all the trouble earlier in the evening.

'That's my business. Now start this thing and let's go.'

When they reached her flat again, both she and Chuck went into the kitchen. Just for a joke, she held up the bottle of Ouzo, raising her brows in a question.

'Are you trying to kill me?' Chuck asked, opening the refrigerator. For a moment she thought he was after a beer, but then he closed the door and gazed at the coffee-pot.

'Choices, choices,' she murmured. 'Have you made one?' That was a loaded question, most of the answers would have been unwelcome.

'Yeah,' he said slowly, still eyeing the pot. A dissatisfaction edged his voice, but it had nothing to do with his thirst. The night was too far advanced, and Barbara felt incapable of tackling any new problems so she decided to forgo any solicitious queries.

While the hot liquid dripped into the glass pot, Barbara went into the bedroom and removed her shoes, returning in a pair of bedroom slippers that were far less glamorous, but much more comfortable. Chuck had taken his customary place on the sofa, his feet propped up on the cushions he kept on the end of the coffee-table. As she passed through the room into the kitchen, he was sitting, his eyes closed, his head back. His expression was not one of triumph over a successful evening, nor had it changed when Barbara returned with the pot and cups on a tray.

She sat down by him and poured. 'I know you were disappointed that we couldn't take the Mercedes, but I don't think anyone saw the truck,' she said, thinking that must be the cause of his unhappiness.

'No, not where we parked it,' Chuck muttered as he sat up and took his cup. 'We could have been driving a battle-ship and no one would have noticed in the rain.'

Obviously that wasn't the problem. Tired or not, Barbara was allowing her concern for him to overcome her fatigue. If he left unhappy, she would worry about it all night.

'I thought we had a very successful day,' she said, hoping that remark would lead somewhere.

'Yes,' he grated, 'And a very successful evening.'

Now she was genuinely puzzled. 'Well, wasn't that the idea—you made friends with some nice people, we played tennis, and you certainly don't have to be ashamed of your game—you played beautifully—'

'So did you.' His compliment shot out like an accusation.

'I was just lucky,' Barbara tried to slide over her game, wondering what could be bothering him. She was fast reaching the conclusion that she was to blame for his mood, but why was still a mystery. Looking back over the evening, she could not think of anything she could have done to put him in a black mood. Perhaps she wasn't as sophisticated as she thought. Had she made some *faux pas*? No, she decided. But she was to blame in some way.

While Chuck absently stirred his coffee, Barbara stared across the room. She would not be able to go with him to the club again, she thought. Not if she had this effect on him. The resolution brought her tears close to the surface. To drive them away she shifted on the sofa cushion and tossed her head.

'Hey, we're forgetting what we're supposed to be doing. Heroes and heroines don't sit around moping into their coffee. They act charming and witty.' She slanted her eyes towards Chuck. 'It's your turn to be charming.'

'Like a cobra?' he demanded.

'What brought on that remark?'

'Never mind.' He rose and crossed the room to the small bookcase near the door. From the top shelf he picked up the book he had bought in that morning and carried it back to the sofa. Barbara watched while he leafed through the pages and dropped it with a hiss of disgust.

'Yeah, that's what you think a man should be—some world traveller, nothing on his mind and on his tongue but where he's been and the glamorous places he's seen.'

'Me?' Barbara gave him a puzzled look. 'This is *me* we're talking about?' Somehow, part of this conversation was passing over her head. Her day had been full, but she wasn't *that* tired. 'If I've done something wrong, I wish you'd tell me what it was.'

'Oh, you didn't do a thing wrong. You were just perfect.' Again Chuck's compliment was thrown like a weapon.

'Then what is it?' By now Barbara was thoroughly confused. As well as puzzled, she was growing irritated. She was chastising herself for ruining his evening, but he wouldn't tell her what was bothering him, so she was flailing herself for nothing. She watched him stirring the coffee. The spoon was grinding against the porcelain. 'And stop stirring that coffee,' she griped. 'You're going to wear out the pattern on the inside of the cup!'

'Why didn't they put the pattern on the outside, then?' Chuck demanded savagely.

'Because it belongs to the inside, just like it's on the

inside of plates,' Barbara answered crossly.

'Dishes must be designed by women,' Chuck said, dropping the spoon in the saucer.

'I doubt it, since most of the patterns were set before women were considered to have any sense.'

'That's a typical female remark.' Chuck frowned across the room for a moment and then turned to gaze at her. 'Is this fight serving any purpose?'

Despite herself, Barbara laughed. They were behaving like children. Two adults should be able to discuss their troubles. The sensible thing for her to do was simply ask him what had bothered him. She did.

'I don't know,' Chuck moved restlessly, trying to cover an obvious dissimulation. 'I guess I feel phony. Tomorrow let's do something else. I don't want to go back to the club.'

'I thought you were having a good time tonight.' Barbara was surprised. He had certainly enjoyed himself, at least up until the last few minutes.

'You certainly did.' Again the accusation.

'There you go again,' Barbara accused in return. 'Why won't you talk about what's bothering you?'

Chuck started stirring the spoon in the half-empty cup. 'I don't feel as if I've anything to talk about. Where have I been? What have I ever done that makes good conversation?'

So that was it. All the talk about travelling and who the Dennises and the Roses had seen had bothered him. Barbara leaned back on the couch and half closed her eyes.

'You mean I don't have to hear about the Jacksons at Cannes, or when you saw the Farringales on the slopes in Switzerland? Do you mean we'd be reduced to subjects we know something about and both have an interest in? How mundane.'

'You were revelling in all that talk,' Chuck looked at her searchingly. Doubt and not a little bit of hope threaded through his voice. 'You certainly looked as if you were.'

'Wasn't I supposed to act as if I were having a good time?' Barbara countered. Actually she *had* enjoyed most of it, but there was a time for that admission and this certainly wasn't it. 'I didn't see you yawning in their faces.'

'Well, I couldn't do that,' Chuck admitted. 'So you weren't really interested either?'

'In people I don't know? Frankly I'd rather talk about Otis. At least I know who he is and what he does. If being a heroic female makes me a heroine, then I made the grade tonight. I put out a superb effort to look happy. I want credit for every bit of it, too.'

'And you should have it,' Chuck leaned over and gave her a kiss on the cheek. Then he drew back. 'Go ahead and say it—how did you rate that—a one?'

'That was definitely a two,' Barbara replied as if soothing his feathers. 'Even I know you can do better than that. You're just tired tonight. You've had a busy day.'

'Yeah, and I think I'll take myself home to bed. See you tomorrow.'

When the door closed behind him, Barbara stood in the hall, not quite sure what had happened. Had she used up the ploy on rating the kisses already? It had seemed so promising. She chewed on her bottom lip as she headed for the bedroom. She needed a new idea, it seemed.

But the situation was looking up. He was not all that happy at the country club, so after the novelty wore off, maybe he would tire of it. That thought was promising. And he was coming tomorrow. When she prepared for bed she picked up the worn copy of *Mediterranean Magic*.

'Come on, Melissa,' she said as she settled herself against the pillows. 'We still have some plotting to do.'

CHAPTER SEVEN

THE next morning Barbara slept later than usual. She awakened with a sense of being behind in her chores, and started right to work. She had showered and washed her hair and was sorting her laundry when the doorbell rang. The cleaners did not deliver on Sunday morning. The visitor could only be Chuck. He had said he would see her that day, but she had not expected him before ten o'clock. Her hair was still uncombed, and the old robe she had put on was not fit for anyone to see.

She rushed into the hall and stood glaring at the door. 'You'll just have to wait a minute!' she shouted before hurrying into the bedroom to dress and comb her hair.

When she opened the door, Chuck was leaning against the wall, his arms folded against his chest. Slowly he held up his watch and inspected it.

'If you think that was a minute, you need a course in telling time,' he said as he walked in.

'And if you think you can walk in on a working girl at this time on Sunday morning when you tied up all her Saturday, you have rocks in your head,' she retorted, closing the door after him.

'I'd rather have those rocks in my stomach,' Chuck answered. 'At least it wouldn't feel so empty. Come on, let's go out for brunch.'

'I need to do my laundry,' Barbara complained. She looked around the room, frowning at the light coating of dust. And she owed her mother a letter.

Chuck sat on the sofa with an air of waiting. 'I don't

know much about those romances, but I bet you can't show me one where the heroine turns down a date because she wants to do laundry.'

'That's a shot below the belt,' Barbara argued.

'Maybe, but glamorous people must do something with their days. Let's get out and find out what it is.'

Barbara gazed at him, feeling her objections die. He was too nonchalant, yet she could hear a trace of urgency underlying what he said. Was he still worried about the talk at the club? she wondered. Apparently the difference in the lifestyles had bothered him. If he was upset, she could forget the laundry. At a pinch she could send her clothes out, she decided.

'Where do you want to go?'

'I don't know.'

'Well, is it casual or dress?' After all, a girl had to have some idea of what to do. Chuck was wearing a shirt and tie, sports coat and slacks.

'Prepare for anything.'

Famous last words, she thought as she headed for the bedroom.

Ten minutes later she was back, wearing a dark blue shantung dress with a matching jacket. The dress had a scooped neckline that set off a gold chain necklace and would be perfect for a dressier atmosphere. The jacket gave it a more casual look. She was glad she had never developed the habit of applying a lot of make-up, and that her hair was an easy-care style. Chuck was pacing the room as if he walked on a hot plate.

'You ready?' He headed for the door as soon as he saw her.

'I think I'd better be or I'd get dragged out in my pyjamas,' she answered as she followed him out.

At the curb she looked up and down the street, wondering what they were using for a vehicle. If Chuck had brought one of the diesel truck cabs, she was not going. It was bad enough to climb up the ladder in darkness, but never in daylight when people might be watching. But she was safe. Little Sadie, her Volkswagen, sat at the curb.

'I thought we'd better trust ourselves to Sadie,' Chuck said as he opened the door. 'At least she keeps on chugging.'

'Didn't you take it apart?' Barbara asked as she settled herself on the seat.

'Uh-huh, and I put it back together,' Chuck said as he climbed in and started the car. 'Something like putting on dirty clothes, but at least we're covered until tomorrow when I can get you a new carburettor.'

Barbara sat back and enjoyed the atmosphere of a San Diego Sunday morning while Chuck babied the little car. He was avoiding the freeways again, so their route took them through Old Town, the original Spanish-American settlement that stood on a naturally gentle slope high above the San Diego Bay. As they travelled the twisted route she caught glimpses of the water, sparkling in the morning sun. The rain the night before had washed the usually clear air. She seemed to be looking through shining crystal that heightened the contrast of the white Spanish-style houses, many with red-tiled roofs. The brilliant shades of bougainvillea, tall poinsettias and huge geranium plants hurled their reds, fuchsias and greens into the sunlight, striking the mind with glory.

As they turned on to San Diego Street, a flood of people were just leaving the large church and Barbara twisted her head to see the children accompanying their parents across the street.

Chuck stopped and waited for a family to cross. Four dark-haired little girls, dressed alike in pink dresses, stair-stepped between their parents as they skipped along in their exuberance.

Barbara cast a look at Chuck under her lashes and was caught by the dreamy, slightly wistful look on his face as he watched the children. She often thought he would make a good father, but it was the first time she had realised he took a conscious pleasure in youngsters. Was Sandy the motherly type? she wondered. She doubted it.

She also doubted Chuck's complaints of hunger as he twisted his way through the city, up and down the steep, San Francisco grades of some of the downtown streets and finally drove into Balboa Park.

'Where are you going?'

'Cafe del Rey Moro,' Chuck replied. 'It's close to the museums, and I thought we might make it a profitable day.'

'Sure,' Barbara agreed, putting a false enthusiasm in her voice. She had been hoping the time spent at the country club, particularly the evening, had dampened his enthusiasm for the project of social polish. Apparently he had decided to try a different tack, but was as determined as ever.

'Did you make a reservation?' Barbara asked. The famous restaurant was usually crowded.

'I did.' Chuck grinned at her. 'I've at least figured out one thing on my own.'

'Don't go putting meanings to my words that aren't there,' Barbara said. 'They're usually so crowded here.'

Their timing was perfect. Chuck gave his name and they were led out to the patio, where they weaved in between the white metal patio chairs and tables, and passed a fountain that busily sprayed its drops into the air. The sparkle of the falling water caught the sunlight and reflected off the wet ivy that grew from a planter in

the centre of the pool. Barbara could not resist pausing
to look for coins, hoping she could also make a donation
to luck and make a wish, but the yellow and blue tiles
that seemed to move with the ripples of the water were
bare.

Just superstition, she chided herself, but she needed all
the help she could get. A little wish, a coin, and a faith in
it might just make the difference, she thought. After all,
Sandy would be returning from her trip in a few weeks,
and once she was back in town, Barbara would be faced
with the truth of her success or failure. With those
thoughts in mind, she hardly noticed the intricacies of
the vines that formed a barrier of shade over their table,
or the startling white columns that held up the lattice
work supporting the greenery. Chuck brought her back
to the present as he looked around, his attention caught
by the activity on a lower terrace. A number of well
dressed people were moving about, and many were
seated on the folding chairs facing the ornate wishing
well.

'Lot of flowers down there—' Chuck looked over the
railing speculatively. 'Hey, it's set up for a wedding! I
forgot they held them here.'

'Me too.' Barbara looked around, wondering if they
were in time for the ceremony. She saw no one obviously
dressed as a participant. But as the waiter brought their
coffee several people entered the grotto from the walk
that skirted the end of the building.

Barbara and Chuck watched the wedding guests
gather as they sat for a bit over their coffee. Since brunch
was a buffet, they re-entered the building and spent
some time on their choices. Barbara, with a weakness
for Chicken Champion and fruit, filled her plate and
followed Chuck back to the table where the waiters
brought them a glass of champagne. They were just

sampling their choices when the groom and the minister took their places. The bride, dressed in white lace, came down the stone path. She moved to the traditional wedding music, but her entry was played by the sweet strings of a harp. The reverberating strings blended with the falling water of the fountain, the eucalyptus trees that formed the natural background seemed to move with the notes that rang liquid in the warm sunny air. Caught by the scene and her own prominent hopes for the future, Barbara watched spellbound as the young woman descended the steps. Her gaze was held by the radiance of happiness on the bride's face. Obviously, she was stepping into a new life full of love and promise. Too full for the slightest doubt to mar the greatest day of her life.

When the bride turned to continue her slow, stately walk to the stone altar, Barbara let out a sigh and only then realised she had been holding her breath. She was a bit ashamed of the envy she felt for the happy young woman. Probing a little deeper into her own thoughts, she realised she did not wish to take one iota of happiness from the bride, but she too longed to make that walk—if Chuck was waiting across the flag-stoned grotto.

No longer able to stand the strain of an onlooker when she herself wanted so desperately to be a part of it, she pulled her attention away, looking first over the patio where the diners watched. Some were caught up in the spell, one couple, who had been ignoring each other, were watching with scornful eyes.

Don't you dare *make fun of their happiness*, she threw the thought across the room at them. Suddenly she wished she could step between them and the view of the wedding party, protecting that fragile happiness below from their sardonic looks.

'Makes you want to jump right up and join them, doesn't it?'

Barbara's mind was jerked back to her own table by Chuck's remark. For a fraction of a second, she wondered if her face had showed her own longing, but after his remark he looked a little ill at ease; he had spoken his own thoughts, and was a bit ashamed of being caught up in the moment. A sudden warmth spread through Barbara. The softness, the sentimentality he had expressed was not consistent with the self-image he was trying to project. Yet he had made his admission to her, trusting her not to use it against him. At that moment she would have given her life to save him from hurt, even if he saw Sandy as the bride walking down the steps.

'Everyone wants that happiness in their lives,' she said thoughtfully, noting her answer had not alleviated his discomfort. 'But it's amazing to me how they can walk down those steps and look so poised. With all those eyes on me, I'd probably stumble over something.'

'Or I'd have to dig your heel out from between the stones,' Chuck laughed as he referred to her getting stuck in the old paving. 'And it's not usual for grooms to carry crowbars in their pockets.'

Around Barbara, the world seemed to tilt. Apparently Sandy had not been in his thoughts, if he saw himself as the groom and Barbara crossing those paving stones. Across the table, he seemed to be having a little trouble with his own balance, at least his mental one. He looked slightly shocked as if he had opened his cupboard door and discovered a world he had not known existed.

Suddenly Barbara was panic-stricken. He never played the ego games, trying for either a physical or emotional seduction just to build himself in his own esteem. If he decided he was leading her to believe in something he was not able to give, he was capable of turning their friendship into one of extreme formality, thinking he was protecting her. Her heart was singing with the knowledge that she was growing in his heart, but for him to discover it too suddenly could put an end to all her hopes.

'Trust you to be around when I need you,' she said lightly, forcing the words around her exultation and her fears. 'But driving a truck and standing up in a morning suit take entirely different kinds of courage. You'd be nothing but a bowl of jelly. You'd need that crowbar to stiffen your backbone.'

'You're crazy,' Chuck retorted. Her teasing insult had caused him to strike out in his own defence. The hazel eyes were lightening to gold as he searched for something witty to counter her remarks.

'Oh, don't tell me you'd be standing down there as calm as that fellow is,' Barbara pressed on.

Chuck raised his eyebrows in true heroic style. 'I can be as calm as a rock,' he insisted. He held out his hand, palm down for emphasis; his little finger just touched the empty champagne glass, turning it over on the table. Chuck stared at it frowning thoughtfully. 'Well—guess I'd better read another book.'

Debilitated with the relief of having his mood restored and the danger past, Barbara could not keep from laughing. Neither could Chuck.

At peace again, they lingered a bit over their coffee until Chuck mentioned the filled tables. 'There's probably a queue of people waiting to get in,' he said regretfully.

Barbara agreed, half resentful that the idyll was broken, but she knew she'd feel guilty if they continued to occupy a table to no purpose, causing others to wait unnecessarily. By his mention of it, Chuck was already feeling the guilt.

Outside the restaurant, they crossed the inner court-yard, taking time to stop and admire another fountain. Here Barbara succumbed to her desire and surrepti-tiously dropped in a coin, watching it sink the few inches to the bottom of the blue-and-yellow tiled pool. As she opened her eyes after making her wish, she thought she imagined a slight smile on the face of the carved female figure that held the jar of pouring water.

'Think it will come true?' Chuck asked with a grin.

'I hope so, or I wouldn't have wished,' Barbara answered, glad he refrained from tossing in a coin. He could laugh at her all he pleased as long as he didn't make a wish that negated hers.

As they walked through the arched entry that led to the small parking lot between the two ornate Spanish-style buildings, Barbara sighed.

'It was wonderful, but I guess it's back to the laundry.'

'What? On a day like this? Forget it,' Chuck de-manded. 'While we're here we might as well absorb some culture.'

'I *have* to do my laundry,' Barbara insisted, stopping in the bright sunlight to frown at him.

'Now *that* is unheroine-ish,' Chuck said grinning. 'I told you, you can't show me a book where the heroine breaks off the romance to go home and wash her stock-ings.' His light tone lost its impact when she saw the determination in his eyes. Why was he adamant about staying in the park?

'You were the one who said those books were fantasy, remember?' Barbara threw his own words back at him. 'But I did read one where a girl stayed at home to wash her hair, doesn't that count?'

Chuck stepped closer, catching a strand of her blonde hair and holding it out in front of her face so she could see three fingers of his hand drawn back as if he were touching something dirty.

'Yuck,' he said, feigning disgust.

'You stop that!' Barbara took a swing at him with her handbag, but expecting it, he bent nearly double, letting her arm pass harmlessly. 'I'll have you know I washed my hair this morning—oh, you rat!' She tried to keep her frown from turning to a laugh as she realised she had fallen into his trap.

'Twice in one day is too much,' Chuck said as he took her arm. 'You'll give it wrinkles from too much water.'

'Where are we going?' Barbara wanted to know as he guided her along the covered walk around the building. The arched columns interspaced with benches and the shrubbery that bordered them created a shaded protected path. Chuck guided her out to the first opening and on to the walk that led to the street.

'I asked you where we were going,' she reminded him.

'To the picture show.' His grin as he brushed his light hair off his forehead made her heart lurch.

But she frowned, puzzled. Did he mean the movies? To her knowledge there wasn't a cinema in the park. The Space Museum had a wonderful film show, but they were going in an entirely different direction. At first she thought he was heading for the Botanical Gardens, but he turned to the left after crossing the street.

She laughed. He was aiming for the Museum of Art. Picture show. Well, she supposed they could call it that.

Inside the lobby, Chuck purchased a catalogue and handed it to Barbara. His attitude said he had bought the tickets and the book, now it was up to her to complete their education.

Barbara opened the guide book and perused it for a few moments. 'If we're going to get anything out of this, we'd better follow the path the book takes,' she suggested.

'Lead the way.'

She led off to the left, entering the first gallery. Several of the paintings in the room were by Toulouse-Lautrec. Chuck walked over to a large street scene, studied it for a moment and then backed up, taking careful steps.

'The farther away you get, the better it looks. From out in La Mesa it's probably gorgeous.'

'Sh-h-h!' Barbara hissed as two elderly, and judging by their expressions, extremely knowledgeable, visitors turned irritated stares on Chuck.

'Well, why didn't he finish painting the faces?' Chuck was belligerent.

'Because he's giving impressions, you idiot,' Barbara whispered. She led the way into another room, hoping, if they skipped a little education here and there, they might stay ahead of the elderly and disapproving couple.

When they came to a stop she found herself staring at another painting she knew would bring out all Chuck's arguments. Like the first, part of the painting was impressionistic, as if a camera had been unfocused.

'You can call it what you want, but it looks to me as if the guy didn't finish the job,' Chuck complained.

'Of course he did,' Barbara replied, not really sure he had, but after all, the museum bought it, so it had to be finished—if it wasn't, the book would have said so, wouldn't it? She started flipping the pages, trying to find out.

Chuck drew back, concentrating hard. 'I don't think he did.' He gave her a look of mild irritation. 'I'm not even sure I like spending the city's money on pictures that aren't finished. Think about it. What if I left your carburettor a blur? You wouldn't go very far.'

'Will you stop that?' Barbara was growing exasperated with his complaining. 'Art is not like mechanics. It's communication, and the artist is saying something to you.'

'And he needs a speech therapist,' Chuck retorted.

'Don't you like any paintings? You just *can't* dismiss them all like that.'

'I don't,' Chuck answered, still with a trace of belligerence. 'I like Rembrandt and some Renoir.'

Fed up, Barbara slapped him smartly on the arm with the catalogue, forcing him to take it or let it fall to the floor.

'You'd better change the way you react, or you'll really be putting your foot in your mouth with that precious country club set.' She walked off to get her temper under control and rounded a corner.

Out of the corner of her eye she could see Chuck, walking slowly, dividing his attention between the catalogue, his progress, so he didn't run into any of the museum's visitors, and searching for her. When he caught her eye his seemed to call her a traitor, walking out on him when he needed her.

Barbara sighed, painting the same label on herself, but knowing there was little she could do. Chuck was a skilled worker. He was logical, precise, and his mind refused to run to the fanciful. He was never going to fully appreciate Van Gogh, and his remark that a Picasso was nothing but an overturned box of children's clippings, was in Barbara's opinion the best explanation of that artist's work ever stated.

Still she stood in front of the work of Peter Hurd, absorbing the fantastic richness of the scene, yet savouring its simplicity. Movement at her shoulder and the rustle of the catalogue warned her Chuck had joined her. After a moment she glanced at him, but for once he wasn't complaining. He was totally absorbed in the wall hanging.

After several minutes he sighed. 'You know, I never get used to that one. I think it's what causes me to dislike so many of the others. That's an artist; he could communicate with skill and precision.'

Barbara gave him a searching look. Then she realised the implications.

'*You* are a fraud,' she announced. 'You're no stranger to the museum.'

He seemed to think that over for a moment. 'No, but I know what I like, and I don't make sense out of half this stuff.' Suddenly his mouth was recalcitrant, trying to curve up at the corners while he tried to keep it straight. 'But I don't speak Dutch either, and there must be some merit in it or people wouldn't raise their kids on it, would they?'

When they left the Museum of Art, they strolled down the street, past the entrance to the Old Globe Theatre, and entered the Museum of Man. They strolled through the artifacts of the Southwest and stopped to stare at the realistic replicas of the Mayan temple gods.

'I don't think I'd like to wake up with that head on the next pillow,' Barbara said as she stared at a large carved stone with a misshapen face filling the entire surface. Since the face was a good six feet wide and more than four feet high, she tried to imagine what size the body would have been, if one had accompanied that head.

'Worse, can you imagine how long it took that guy to shave?'

The image of a giant with a safety razor caused Barbara to giggle. She tried to keep from laughing aloud, but, suppressed, the spasms shook her entire body. She heard a snort of outrage and turned to see the couple from the Museum of Fine Art standing behind them. Suddenly it was impossible to hold in her laughter, even with both hands over her mouth. Mercifully Chuck caught her arm and pulled her away.

'I'm sorry,' she said between gasps when they were outside. Blotting away the tears, she explained her mental picture of the giant and the safety razor to Chuck. '. . . and when I saw those people who have no sense of humour at all—' She paused, not really clear on how to explain how they added to the picture, but Chuck seemed to know. His laugh was louder than hers.

'I'll tell you what, let's go and listen to the organ recital. Maybe we can reconstruct our decorum, and I guarantee the two frowners won't be there. No Brahms today.'

'If there's Brahms, I don't want to go.' Barbara loved classical music, but not Brahms.

'No Brahms, I read the programme.' Chuck pulled a paper out of his pocket, and Barbara saw it was a list of park activities for that particular day.

Her laundry was still waiting, but she wasn't going to argue. Heroines never had aching feet in the books she read, but then, by the time they were in a book, they were fully rated in their roles. She was still a trainee. And she was bothered by Chuck's attitude. He was searching for something to occupy their time. He didn't seem over-excited about their activities, so why was he sticking with them?

In front of the beautiful Spanish-style organ pavilion, the benches held several hundred people as the city organist did his stuff. His programme was light, bringing back memories of old songs and the crowd, sitting in the sunshine, was appreciative. The curving wings of the pavilion made an arched, covered walkway. They had been fortunate in their seats. The shadow of a portico fell across them and they listened to the lively music without having to worry about the heat of the sun.

When the programme was over and the audience

stood for applause, Barbara looked warily at Chuck.

'Do I get to do my laundry now?'

Chuck frowned. 'What is this with laundry? Are you telling me I don't rate above a pile of dirty clothes? Come on, there's somewhere I want to go.'

Barbara followed him down the row of benches, and out on to the pavement. She waited until they were away from most of the crowd before she gave him an answer.

'I hate to tell you this, Buddy, but there is a difference between heroes and heroines.'

'You mean like the difference between little boys and little girls? Tell me all about it.'

'No,' Barbara shook her head, refusing to allow herself to be baited into losing her train of thought. 'I mean about what you wear. Fellows can stuff shirts and socks into bags and send them to the laundry. Hero-ine-ish—' Her tongue tangled over Chuck's newly coined word. 'Heroineish clothes have to have delicate care.'

'Are you going to be a spoilsport?' Chuck asked, his expression obstinate. Barbara wondered why.

'No,' Barbara was reluctant with her answer. 'I guess you rate a little above the laundry, at least in my book.'

'Thanks a lot.'

Chuck's destination was Spanish Village. The little cluster of craft shops could have been a small village in Mexico or Spain except for the numbers of people that filed through the shops and in the paved square.

In one of the galleries, Chuck paused, and Barbara, waiting out in the square, stood for a while. Then she entered. She was surprised to find him standing in front of a painting after his reaction to the work in the museum. Since he seemed to resent anything that wasn't totally classical, she wondered that he would be interested in what she first took to be a collage.

Not until she stepped up behind him did she see her

mistake. The painting was so technically accurate it could have been a series of photographs, simply the heads of musicians and singers, yet there was such life, such purpose in the faces that they were more a kaleidoscope of musical excitement. She didn't need the title, 'Jazz Musicians,' to tell her about their music. It played on her mind, as it had played on the heart of the painter, Mark Rauschwald. She noted the name for future reference.

'See,' Chuck muttered as he realised she had joined him. 'It is possible to combine skill and complete communication. My foot wants to tap.'

Barbara, nodded and moved away, looking at the other work. She let Chuck go one direction and she went another. While he was busy looking at primitive sculptures, she stepped outside and sat on one of the benches under the shade trees that interrupted the sun of the square.

By now she was beginning to fret. The sun was moving across the horizon. Not being able to do her laundry had escaped to the back of her mind. Instead she was wondering what possessed Chuck to remain in the park all day. In the year and a half she had known him, he had not evidenced any great urge to saturate himself in the atmosphere of the famous place. He was usually tired at weekends and wanted to spend his Sundays resting for the week ahead.

True, the business pressures had been overwhelming, and had only eased off in the past few weeks, but this change was a little abrupt. Possibly she was just beginning to think about it because she was tired. During the early part of the day she had just been so glad to be with him, the change from his usual interest hadn't bothered her. Maybe she noticed it because she was tired.

'And hungry,' she said aloud.

'Me too,' Chuck answered, seeming to think nothing of her abrupt statement.

'Culture—what the beautiful people do—' Barbara muttered as they walked away from the small village and took the paved path that would take them back towards the car. 'We certainly didn't take full advantage of what was around us today.'

'We had a good time,' Chuck countered, not a bit abashed because they listened to semi-popular music instead of the classical, or his critical remarks about the famous artists in the museum.

Dinner could not have been called culturally uplifting. They bought hot dogs covered with chili from a park cart and sat on a bench, watching the shadows of the eucalyptus trees creep across the lawn and up the sides of the buildings.

Under her lashes, Barbara looked at Chuck as he concentrated on his food and stared out over the park. He appeared to be happy, content. She wondered if he were thinking of Sandy, but decided he was not. Neither relaxation nor contentment was normal for him when the sultry socialite was on his mind. He was either intensely happy, or worried and harried. There had never been a mid-way in his feelings for her.

Barbara thought back to the conversation over brunch when he had startled himself and her by mentally replacing the bride and groom with himself and Barbara. Did that mean anything? She decided it did, otherwise he would not have been so shocked by the knowledge. That little slip did prove he cared, she decided. Her plan was beginning to work, but did she have enough time to bring it to fruition? She knew she had to move slowly. The idea had to grow so slowly on his mind that his feelings were deeply rooted and in flower before he realised it. Moving too fast would destroy everything.

She needed more romantic situations, nothing he would notice. She looked up at the darkening sky, punctuated by the lights on the park streets. Evening was a good time for—

'Romance,' Chuck said suddenly. Barbara almost tumbled off the bench. Had she been thinking aloud? She stared at him wide-eyed, too startled and embarrassed to speak.

'That's what we've been missing today,' Chuck said, frowning at her, letting her know it was her fault. 'It's all that talk about laundry. You shouldn't be talking about laundry when you're out with a man. That's not romantic.'

Almost light-headed after her fright, Barbara could not contain the humour of having her thoughts so abruptly spoken by Chuck. She twisted her position so she faced him squarely.

'Then show me romance.' She pursed her lips and pushed them out until they resembled the mouth of a chimpanzee or a duck's bill. From her position she wasn't sure which.

'Yuck.' Chuck shook his head and pushed at her. 'That's the wrong method, lady. I rate that as a minus forty-five.'

'Then show me.' Afraid she had been a little too forward for her purpose, she jumped up and walked a few feet away to inspect a carving on the trunk of a eucalyptus tree.

Chuck came to stand beside her, his hands in his pockets, his head down, as if studying the ground. 'That's what's wrong,' he said quietly. 'I don't think I know what "romantic" really means.'

Barbara gave up her inspection of the tree and let him lead. He was walking aimlessly, she knew, but they were heading for the high bridge that crossed the freeway and led to the other side of the park. She strolled along beside him.

'First, it has to come out of yourself,' Barbara said, putting her thoughts into words, all the time knowing she was not experienced enough to be an expert, yet she had some definite feelings on the matter when he brought up the subject. 'I think, first you have to want romance, and then you make the most of your opportunities.'

'That's going to take some thinking,' Chuck replied.

They crossed the long bridge in silence. Barbara didn't look at Chuck again. Instead she thought about what she had said. She needed the answers. Take advantage of the opportunities around her.

Take advantage of your opportunities—

They reached the end of the bridge. To the right, across the street, the many varieties of plant life created almost a Persian Paradise. On their left shrubbery gave way to a wide grass lawn, occasionally interrupted by large shade trees. Chuck chose the path of least resistance and turned left.

Barbara walked at his side, thinking about the books she had read.

Take advantage of your opportunities—

The thought kept running through her mind.

They were walking close to the oleander bushes that masked the hill and the freeway from sight. Occasionally she heard the buzz of some nocturnal insect, and around them was the constant sound of chirping crickets. Barbara heard a rustling in the bushes and dismissed it, knowing it was only a dog.

Take advantage of your opportunities—

She decided she was being idiotic. Several months ago she had read a romance that ended happily because of some creature in the bushes. The heroine had become so frightened she fainted, falling into the hero's arms. He had been so concerned and protective he realised at last he loved her.

Of course, that heroine had reason to be frightened. She had been in the wilds of Africa. The creature in the bushes had been a lion. Barbara frowned, then smiled slyly. She could make believe the dog was a lion, couldn't she? After all, the zoo helped to make Balboa Park world famous. She could think it was an escaped lion.

Her practical mind wondered how, if a lion did escape, it could get across the freeway without being noticed, but she pushed that aside. Logic she didn't need.

All she needed to do was wait for the dog to rustle the bushes again, and she would swoon into Chuck's arms. That should certainly start something.

She edged closer to Chuck who was still walking, head down, as he thought. She waited until the dog, a co-operative creature, if it was a dog, rustled the bushes again, this time much closer to them. Perfect. Caught up in her own ploy, she barely heard and paid no attention to a gasp from Chuck.

'Oh-h-h,' she quavered, or hoped it was quavering. She raised one hand to her forehead, swaying towards Chuck as she let go of her balance. The bottom dropped out of her plan as no strong arms grasped her. She glimpsed Chuck, turned half away as she struck the ground.

The fall had knocked the breath out of her, but in a moment she realised she was uninjured, and started to sit up. Chuck was hopping around in a circle, slapping at his leg. He paused only for a moment when he saw her lying on the ground.

'What are you doing?' he demanded. His voice was as

close to panic as she had ever heard and he was slapping at his right leg, but at the moment she had grievances of her own.

'I was fainting,' she yelled at him. 'And any fledgling hero worth his salt would have caught me!'

'Not with a bug up his trouser leg!' Chuck yelled back. 'Besides, that wasn't in the book!'

Barbara sat still, fearing she had ruined her dress with grass stains, and afraid to move, because if the dress was still unmarked, she might do it irreparable damage. And at the moment she had no desire to help Chuck with his problem. She was fed up.

'Not everything in life was in that book,' she said, her voice raised to penetrate his concentration on his hopping and slapping.

'Are you folks having trouble?'

Barbara looked around to see a policeman standing on the grass, his arms akimbo as he watched Chuck's choreography, letting his gaze wander back and forth to Barbara, still half prone on the ground.

Still too upset by her failure to be prudent, she glared up at the officer. 'And *you* weren't in the last two books either!' she told him, making part of the fault his by implication. In her state of mind she wasn't bothered by taking Chuck's side of the argument. He was still too busy beating on his trouser leg to pay much attention.

Gazing at her speculatively, the policeman pushed back his cap and considered the situation. Barbara could almost read his mind in the expressions that moved across his face. It was Sunday afternoon, and he didn't need a hassle. Two nuts like these would probably have to be hauled in with the wagon. He'd be up half the night making reports. There was probably no law against rain-dancing in the park anyway, as long as they didn't draw a crowd.

He pulled his hat back in line.

'Lady, by the time the next edition comes out, I hope I'll be on holiday.' The officer pointed an accusing finger at Chuck. 'But if that rain-dance works, he could get sued.' He turned and walked away, disappearing into the shadows.

Barbara looked back at Chuck who had slowed his antics and was shaking the leg of his trousers. A dead cricket fell out on to the grass. Like Chuck she leaned forwards to inspect the poor mangled insect.

'Do you mean you let me fall on the ground for that?' she demanded.

'I didn't know what that was,' Chuck retorted.

'Poor little thing, all it did was jump,' Barbara said, still staring at the dead cricket. 'Crickets are supposed to jump, that's why they have long back legs. And you go and kill it.'

'You're not mad about the cricket,' Chuck accused. 'You're just uptight because I didn't catch you, and how was I to know you'd start flopping all over the ground?'

'Flopping?' Barbara forgot her concern for a dress and jumped to her feet. 'Of all the inconsiderate—' She turned on her heel and started for the bridge, her route back to the car.

'Wait a minute,' Chuck trotted to keep up. 'Don't jump on me. It wasn't all my fault, you know.'

'Oh, wasn't it?' Barbara was too angry to think straight. From overhead they heard the ominous roll of thunder.

'Now look what you did!' she yelled at him as she sprinted across the bridge, trying to outrun the rain. The cop had called it rain-dancing, and apparently he knew.

Chuck ran behind her.

'Well, at least I learned something,' he shouted, half in anger, half in triumph.

CHAPTER EIGHT

TORN between excitement and curiosity, Barbara expected to have a hard time sleeping that night. What had possessed Chuck to be so demanding of her time that day? He certainly had not cared for the museums, they had done nothing to strengthen their 'cultural experience,' as she had expressed it on the way home, yet every time she had mentioned cutting the park visit short, he had become more insistent that they continue.

And what about that slip he made when they were talking about the wedding? Did it really mean anything, or was she building it up in her mind, just looking for hope where none existed? She warned herself not to build on a chance statement made in the spirit of the moment, and totally without meaning. His startled look probably came from wondering if she had put an importance to it that had not existed in his mind when he spoke.

It was natural enough for him to include her in his thoughts, especially since they spent so much time together.

Don't read in hope that will come to nothing but heartbreak, she kept telling herself.

Her mind might be in a tumble, but her body was physically tired. She drifted off to sleep and her subconscious mind had not heard one doubt. She dreamed she was walking those brick stairs down to the wishing-well. Her dress was white lace. The minister and Chuck waited for her at the bottom. Chuck had a crowbar in his back pocket. The curved end of the heavy metal tool stuck up over his shoulder as if he were holding Little Bo Peep's sheep crook behind him.

Chuck wasn't at the office when she arrived at work. The note on her desk told her he had been in, but left again to get the carburettor for her Volkswagen. She made the coffee, opened the mail and was working on the files when she heard him drive in. The sound of the jeep was unmistakable.

At noon, Little Sadie purred in her VW accent as he drove it up to the door, raced the engine for her to hear, and parked it in its accustomed place.

Barbara poured his coffee and had it waiting when he entered the office.

'Payment on account, sir,' she said as she handed him the cup.

'And you can tell me how smart I am,' Chuck grinned as he flopped in a chair.

'Just absolutely brilliant, probably the only man in the world who can discuss Renoir and replace carburettors.' Barbara, like Chuck, was in a good mood, and the game made the slow start of the day more interesting.

'And can do rain-dances,' he reminded her. 'Don't forget the rain-dancing.'

Barbara was ready with an answer, but she was prevented from giving it by the ringing phone. She picked up the receiver, answering with the company name.

'You're a hard person to catch.' Like many good secretaries and Girl Fridays, she had developed the ability to recognise voices on the phone. The caller was Jim Dennis.

'Good morning, Mr Dennis,' she replied, wondering what his opening statement meant. She wondered what an advertising firm might want to ship, but he could be recommending them for some large job. The thought made her smile and she looked over at Chuck, crossing her fingers in a silent wish. She was puzzled by the glower he returned.

'I tried to call you several times yesterday,' Jim said. 'I had hoped we could have dinner last night.'

'You tried to call me—here?' Certainly he knew the office would be closed on Sunday.

'No, of course not. At your home. I got the number from Chuck on Saturday night. Wasn't that okay?'

'Oh—yes,' Barbara said, staring at her boss with narrowed eyes. Suddenly, she knew what had upset him that night at the club and the activities of the previous day made sense. He wanted to keep her from going out with Jim Dennis, and the day spent in the park had been his way of trying to prevent it.

Pleading a sudden influx of work at the office, Barbara stalled Jim, telling him she would have to wait until later in the week to make any social plans. She managed to end the call gracefully.

When she put down the phone Chuck was on his way to his office.

'Come back here!' she demanded, trying to hide her amusement.

'I've got work to do,' Chuck objected, but he turned back to the chair with a defensive tenseness in his shoulders.

'Why didn't you tell me you gave Jim Dennis my telephone number?'

'You don't want to go out with him. He's a wolf.'

Barbara bit her lips to keep from laughing. Chuck was right, of course. She had seen the looks that passed between the romantic lupine and the women at the country club, and obviously not all the females had been single. She really had no interest in Jim, but Chuck's machinations to keep them apart struck her as funny.

But the concern Chuck was showing could be a distinct advantage, she decided. She let her eyes widen innocently.

'Why, how can you say that? He seemed like a perfectly nice person.' Did she sound as phony to him as she did to herself? Maybe she should take a course in dissimulation.

Chuck's eyes darkened as he stood looking down at her. 'Jim Dennis is not your type,' he said. 'You can do better than him.'

'Well, recent history doesn't show that,' Barbara remarked. 'He's the first man to come into my orbit in some time. Maybe I'd better grab while I can.'

Be careful, she warned herself. She would do serious damage to her plans if she made her statements irrevocable. Chuck could only be pushed so far.

'We'll find you someone better than him,' Chuck snapped. He stood flat-footed, but indecisive, adamant, yet not sure in what direction to take the conversation.

We already have, you just don't know about it, Barbara thought. Like Chuck, she was not sure what to say next. They were both removed from the necessity by the telephone as it stridently broke into their discomfort.

Barbara hesitated before she picked up the phone, but decided Jim Dennis was unlikely to call twice in so short a time. With more confidence she reached for it, identified the company and as she listened her eyes widened.

'Oh, yes, if you'll wait just a moment I'll check his schedule. I'm sure we can work in an appointment sometime this week.' Pushing the hold button, she looked up at Chuck, her eyes alight. 'Would you have any free time for a meeting with the transportation manager of Samuels and Company?'

'Give me three minutes!' Chuck nearly spilled his coffee as he jerked from his flat-footed stance to lean forward over the desk. 'Not really,' he said, recognising his initial excitement as unprofessional. But the Samuels contract was a large one, and would boost the small trucking company into the middle range.

Barbara looked at her watch. Chuck would have to shower and change, then drive to the large manufacturing company offices.

Chuck's look turned panicky. 'It has to be today! I've got that long run this week. Say—two o'clock.'

When Barbara spoke to the secretary from Samuels and Company for the second time, she was slightly hesitant. 'Mr Ingram is tied up for the rest of the week, but he is free this afternoon—would it be possible that—very good, would two—oh, yes, he could just make a one-o'clock appointment. Yes, he's free for lunch.'

Barbara hung up the receiver, jumped up from her desk and danced a little jig. She managed only a few steps behind her desk before Chuck caught her arm and pulled her out into the open area in the middle of the room. They both tried a little rain-dancing.

'We're on our way!' Barbara sang.

Chuck stopped the cavorting first. 'Should I make reservations at the club for lunch? I think I should.'

'I'll make them,' Barbara rounded her desk again, reaching for the phone. She stopped, her hand halfway towards the instrument. 'You didn't have time to tune up the Mercedes—' she wailed. 'Why didn't you leave Sadie alone and fix the other car?'

For a moment Chuck looked wistful. Then his face cleared. 'Little Sadie—I'll take her if you don't mind.'

That settled, Chuck headed for the back of the building, shouting over his shoulder what a bright guy he was for keeping the full bathroom with a shower when he renovated the building for an office. His bragging was an outlet for his high spirits and higher hopes. Barbara heard every word, feeling their sparkle as if they had been jewels falling from a pirate's treasure chest.

The reservation at the club made, she went back to sorting her files, feeling childish as she arranged a series of empty manila folders with the name Samuels block-printed in large black letters. But silly though they might look, they were her contribution in hope for the brightening future of the company.

When Chuck came from his office, dressed in a dark blue tailored suit, he stood behind her as she carefully aligned the files in the drawer. His hand, coming down on her shoulder, was her first knowledge of his reappearance, and she felt doubly the fool because he saw what she was doing. She looked up shyly, doubtfully, wondering if he would make fun of her, but his eyes were soft, sympathetic.

'If we don't get the contract, it won't be your fault,' he said softly. 'I've got to go—how about a kiss for luck?'

She turned, moving into his arms as if her entire life had been aimed towards that one destination. His lips, unparted, came to meet hers. The gentle touch, a communication of their combined hopes, was far more valuable at the moment than the most urgent desire. More important was the closeness, the togetherness that combined their dual consciousness towards their goal.

Chuck drew back, his eyes soft but laughing. 'You can call that a two if you want, but it won't knock down my elation at the moment.' He turned and rushed out to the yard.

Barbara caught her breath and dashed to the door, catching it just before it closed.

'That was a ten!' she shouted after him.

The Volkswagen door was just closing, but he heard her and waved.

When he drove out of the yard, Barbara returned to her desk. Deliberately she pushed the small pile of correspondence to the side and put her elbows on the desk, her hands clasped to hold her chin. She was preparing for some concentrated dreaming.

Their first really large contract—if Chuck won it, and she had complete faith in his abilities—they were on their way to success. Samuels and Company would be happy with their service, and that would lead to more. Word of satisfaction had a way of spreading. She imagined her desk stacked high with invoices and bills of lading; they would need another filing-cabinet and someone else to help out in the office. That dreamed up necessity brought a pang of regret. Another person in the office meant the privacy they enjoyed would be at an end.

Maybe success was not so great after all, she thought, and was ashamed of herself. She was thinking selfishly. To keep their privacy, would she be willing to hold Chuck back, to keep him from gaining the success he worked so hard to attain? She knew she wouldn't. But a darker spectre loomed up. The growth of the business would be dangerous to her romantic plans. His growing success would make him more attractive to Sandy.

Barbara had been counting on Sandy's ingrained snobbery. She was hoping Sandy would stop and think, realise how it would sound to her friends when she said her husband owned a small trucking company, and shy away from the idea. Owning a large and profitable business would put Chuck in a different position.

But she would have to live with that, she decided. She would not hinder his success, even if she had the opportunity. Resolutely she turned back to the typewriter and pounded out the correspondence. By two o'clock the envelopes were addressed, the quick trip down to the corner letter box had sent them on their way, and she had nothing to do.

She had just pulled *Mediterranean Magic* from her purse and started to read when the phone rang.

Breathlessly she grabbed the receiver, thinking Chuck had been too excited to give her the good news in person. But the caller was Jim Dennis. She was slightly irritated at the disappointment, but tried to keep it from showing.

She kept her feelings out of her voice, and as a result, she realised her false warmth was almost a come-on as she told him how much she regretted not being able to go out with him and a group of his friends. Dinner on a yacht might be interesting, she told herself when she hung up the phone, but she would rather share the evening with Chuck.

If he got the contract, he would want to celebrate. If he didn't get it—she didn't want to think about his disappointment. But he would need her then, even if she was only a sounding board for his frustration. She couldn't just walk off and leave him alone on this important night.

But at five-thirty she wondered if she had made a mistake in turning down Jim's invitation. Chuck had not returned to the office. He had not called. Did he forget she too would be on edge, waiting to hear? Since he had taken Little Sadie she searched his desk for an extra set of keys to the jeep, locked up the office and went back to her quiet flat.

She had just finished a bologna sandwich and a glass of cream soda when the loud knocking on the door caused her to jump. Her hand was still on the knob when Chuck strode in, his suit jacket open and pushed back, his hands stuffed in his pockets—his usual stance when he was pleased with himself. His grin could have split his face.

'You did it!' she breathed a whisper, afraid to speak out loud for fear she might jinx their hopes before he confirmed it.

'We got it!' Chuck's near-shout made up for her lack of volume. He swung her around the narrow hall until they both bumped into the wall. 'All we can handle right now, and on sixty-day notice we can take on more work.' He pulled her towards the kitchen and opened the refrigerator door, bending to look inside.

When he raised his face, he looked like a child who'd lost his candy. 'I know we bought a bottle of champagne to celebrate—'

Barbara knelt beside him. 'There it is, hiding behind that large box of biscuits.'

'You're the only person I know who keeps biscuits in the refrigerator,' Chuck grumbled. But minor irritations had no place with him. He talked steadily as Barbara reached for the glasses and he opened a champagne bottle.

'I thought they just wanted someone to haul their overload, because they have their own trucks and drivers.' He paused to carry the bottle and the glasses in the living-room and put them on the coffee-table in front of the couch. Barbara followed, waiting as he filled her glass and placed it on the table, clearly expecting her to sit by him. She did as he continued.

'But it seems they want to get out of the trucking end of the business altogether. If I can come up with enough vehicles and drivers in time, we can double and triple the initial contract.'

'Marvellous,' Barbara answered. And it was marvellous. But a quaking shiver went through her as she considered the money he would need to keep buying trucks. Even second-hand, they were unbelievably costly. The only fast source of capital that came instantly to mind was Sandy.

She sipped her champagne and stared across the room. Why, suddenly, when everything was going so great, did every action seem to clear a path for the socialite and leave Barbara out in the cold?

Chuck kept babbling about his day, what he had seen at Samuels and Company, how the platform was easy to load from—what was the difference in platforms? Barbara wondered. They were all the same height, she was sure. But Chuck was for the moment in love with the company whose business would allow him to take a giant step into his dreams. She forced all her fears away. He brought his happiness, wanting to share it with her. He was giving her a precious gift. She had no right to cheapen it with fears and jealousy.

'You're going to be rich, important and powerful,' she said.

Chuck's laugh was sudden and filled with heady delight. 'Here's to rich and powerful,' he said, raising his glass. 'And important—wonder how it feels to be important?' The glasses clinked as they touched them together. Barbara took a sip from hers. As if to insure the future truth of the toast, Chuck drained his. Barbara refilled it.

'Before I know it, you'll be in all the papers and running for Congress or something.'

Chuck shook his head. 'I'll be running from one truck to another, trying to make sure all the drivers show up and the brakes work. Can you imagine, if we had twenty trucks, what a time I'd have trying to keep them all tuned up?'

'The price of success,' she quipped.

'To the price of success,' Chuck retorted. The glasses

clinked again. Again Chuck drained his glass. Barbara wondered at the amount of champagne he was drinking, but after all, this was his first large triumph in the business world. She fully expected him to have many more, but he must be allowed to enjoy this one. She refilled his glass again, determined not to say anything that would dampen his exultation.

And she was happy with his last remark. He would be the same Chuck, she thought, even if the company became one of the largest in the country. As it grew he would be forced to hire someone else to service the trucks, but his question revealed something vital in his character. He would still want to do the work himself. His self-image would remain that of a worker, a man who took more pleasure in labour well done than in the power to order others around. Sandy would have a hard time overcoming that.

'And you'll need an office staff of fifty,' Barbara said, leaning back and playing with the glass in her hand as she exaggerated the dream. 'You won't even know the names of your employees.'

'Oh, that will be your job,' he said expansively. 'You can keep them all in order. I can just see you, sitting behind a desk in a big office, glasses down on your nose, as you look over the monthly reports.'

'Monthly reports? Why do I have to read them? What are you going to be doing?'

'Waiting for you to come in and brief me, of course. I'm a big shot, you know. No trivialities. Here's to being a big shot.' The third toast emptied his glass again. When Barbara filled it she added to her own, which was still half full.

'And I'm supposed to sharpen your pencils, I suppose?' The remark was silly since she always kept the writing materials on his desk in perfect order.

'Certainly not. We'll hire a pencil sharpener.' He leaned back and dropped one arm carelessly around her shoulders. 'You'd better make a list, you'll want some-one to change the ribbons on your typewriter too.'

'No typewriter, I want a computer.'

'One computer coming up. Just one, or one for each hand?'

'One for each employee. I'm managing fifty people, remember? I don't have time to do any work. Not if I look after them and brief the boss. Wait a minute—fifty one, we'll have to get you a full-time private caddy for your golf clubs.'

Chuck was quiet for a moment. Then his eyes, nearly gold in his excitement, were turned on her, the laughter barely hidden.

'Tell me, company manager, where are we going to put those fifty-one people?'

'We'll put up shelves in my office, and several little lifts.'

'That's what I like, a manager that manages.' He leaned forward slightly and gave her a kiss on the cheek.

Barbara was careful to keep her movements non-chalant as she reached over to put the champagne glass back on the table. But when she relaxed against the cushions again, she was a bit closer, slightly more shel-tered in the curve of his arm as it lay across the back of the sofa. She had tried to push away the fears that built during the afternoon, but they kept nagging, trying to pull away her self-confidence.

Would his victory that day bring many changes? A few would be inevitable. How many she was afraid to think of. They were joking when they spoke of fifty people, but would they really need to increase their office staff? Not if she could help it. Chuck would have to start driving for a week or so if they started picking up from

Samuels and Company right away. She sighed.

He had been staring across the room and beyond, looking into the future too, but her sigh brought him back. His arm slid from the back of the sofa to rest on her shoulders. With his fingers he lightly caressed her, a soothing gesture.

'Poor Babs,' he soothed. 'This may be a big step for the company, but it will mean more work for you for a while. Do you mind handling some of the routing? I'll have to drive until I find a couple of good men.'

'I can do it,' she answered. He was confirming her fears, but she felt a warmth in thinking how close their thoughts matched. Her answer had sounded a little cocksure though. 'You've talked to me about it often enough.'

'Too much?' he asked softly. 'Don't you sometimes get bored with all my yack about the company?'

'Get bored?' she turned her blue eyes on him in surprise. 'How could I be bored? Making the company a success is what we want—how can I help if you don't talk to me, teach me—how would I learn otherwise? I *love*—' she floundered, catching herself just before she said *I love you and anything you want to do.* 'I love the company, and I want its growth.' Her last sentence was lame, a limping cover for the reason behind her affection for the company.

His right arm tightened around her, pulling her closer. His left hand came around to meet his right, putting a circle of protection around her.

'Then what is it? Something is scaring you—' His eyes searched her face, their expression showed his concern, a little patient humour. 'Don't tell me it isn't. I know you too well.'

The protection provided by his arms alleviated the need for the self-protection she had been building. Part of the truth came pouring out. She spoke haltingly, not wanting to destroy the triumph of the day, yet he wouldn't be satisfied with anything less than the truth.

'There will have to be other people,' she mumbled. 'Maybe not right now, but later. It's been so nice, the two of us—hoping—planning—somehow when a dream comes true something ends up missing after that—' She faltered into silence. Nothing she was trying to say came out right.

'Like the time I dreamed for six months about inviting Mary Johnson to a dance when I was in the seventh grade—' Chuck said slowly.

Barbara looked up, wondering what Mary Johnson had to do with her feelings, but Chuck went on.

'I was thirteen—that dance was held the last Saturday night of the school year and it was our first step into the adult world. When she accepted, my success brought me all sorts of comp—complications. Mom took me to buy a new suit, and new shoes—I had to miss a baseball game for that. My allowance wouldn't cover taking out girls, so I started mowing the neighbours' lawns. I guess I'm saying it just brought other complications. It always happens that way.'

Barbara remained silent. He did understand. Intuitively he had heard more of her fears than his conscious mind had picked up, otherwise his comparison would not have been an affair of the heart. His arms tightened around her.

'Maybe I'm wrong—I'm prejud—prejudging,' he said slowly. 'But I think, if we had fifty people, it wouldn't make any difference with us. You and I will still be dreaming—still be making the plans. They'll be somewhere on the outside, just physical evidence that some of our plans came out right.'

Barbara ducked her head to wipe away a tear. With it

went all the doubts. He had known how to get to the core of her problems and had banished them into the world of the forgotten. Wearied with her worries, when he pulled her head down onto his shoulder, she let it rest there, feeling safe and secure. When the vision of Sandy flitted through her mind, she dismissed it. Sandy would never share those dreams and hopes as Barbara had and would. She refused to let any other fears crop up. He had said all the others would be on the outside. So would Sandy, in a manner of speaking. She would put herself there with her selfishness and her lack of interest, but outside she would be.

They sat quietly for some minutes, then Barbara realised her mood and feelings were subtly changing. Chuck had been stroking her shoulder much like an adult calming a child, but slowly the caress had changed into a communication more adult-to-adult and sensual. The tips of his fingers were sensitising her flesh, sending small trills of feeling through her body. She raised her head, wondering how to respond, and felt the sensations of desire double within her as she met his eyes. They had darkened with urgency. His lids were half closed, his lips parted as she gazed at him.

The raising head had been a signal with him. He half twisted, turning her as he did; his lips met hers and all semblance of two friends fell away. Suddenly they were fated lovers, their lips and their bodies meeting. His arms tightened around her, she clung to him. All the longings, all the achings of every woman that had ever loved were in her arms as she clutched at him, begging to be taken, both physically and emotionally.

His lips explored hers, his tongue, a flicking tool of rising desire, searched her mouth and found the soft sensuous places that sent waves of passion through her body. His kiss awakened every loved-starved nerve. She gripped him tighter, moaning in her pleasure and the pain of her ecstasy as if vessels long unused were filling beyond capacity, stretching her inner being. He correctly interpreted the sound escaping from her throat and put a new intensity into his kiss. His tongue burrowed deeper seeking the hidden spots, awakening more of her than she had known existed.

When he drew back, she wanted to cry out for the loss, to scream against a fate that tortured her with unrelenting vengeance. But if it thwarted her, he too felt its push. Like Barbara, Chuck was shaken. His breath came rasping through his slightly parted lips. He trembled slightly with his desire. As his eyes held hers she viewed a new Chuck. The primordial drive of his passion flamed in his eyes. It held her fascinated with a strength she had not anticipated. She feared it slightly, yet was drawn by it. She sat, feeling like the bird, hypnotised by the cobra, yet something in her revelled in the inability to escape, to know surrender was the only possible course. He read the answer, the capitulation in her gaze. His flickering lids, the slight movement of his mouth showed he accepted and triumphed in his victory.

Wordlessly they remained only inches apart for moments that dragged against the edge of urgency. Then together they defied fate and won. The mutual force of their arms around each other, the desire that pulled them together, was a bruising contact, short-lived and fiery. Barbara felt the breath forced out of her, and knew her contribution was less in strength than in will.

Then Chuck's mouth left hers. His lips travelled over her cheek, found the sensitive areas on her neck. The unceasing movement of his tongue awakened new areas of sensation, of delight.

'Such beautiful skin,' he murmured. She felt the flutter of his lashes beneath her chin as he teased the hollow of her throat. He brought out shivers of pleasure as his ragged breath added a sensuality of its own.

His movement was so skilful she hardly realised it when he bent over her, forcing her backwards with a velvet strength until she was lying on the sofa. He stretched out beside her, one arm circling her back, his lips on hers as his right hand caressed her arm, her shoulder, and his fingers caught in her hair.

He raised his head and carefully ran his fingers through the uneven blondness. Then he took a strand and, using it as an instrument of desire, trailed the end along her cheek bone. The fine strands were feather-light as he drew them across her quivering lips, down on her chin and teased the skin on her throat.

'Spun moonlight,' he said; his voice was a little slurred.

'Spun of dreams come true,' she murmured and turned her head, seeking his lips. His met hers, a long lingering kiss that pulled at her core, demanded a full release, a giving in return. Her hands kneaded the muscles on his back, feeling them cord as he pulled her to him. She was lost in the embrace when reality came slowly back. Chuck was gradually pulling away.

'What is it?' She whispered as she buried her face in his neck. She wanted to hide away, knowing what he would say, yet desperately wanting to negate it.

'Thish isn't r-right—' he spoke slowly as if the words were being forced out of him. She had known, from the moment he started withdrawing what he would say. Her mind set up a wail. He wanted to be a hero out of a story book, but he'd tangled his books. He was supposed to be a romantic hero, not a knight. For a moment she railed against his sense of honour that kept him from her. Her entire body added a chorus as her nerves vibrated with a desire that was to remain unfulfilled.

She lay unmoving, hoping he would forget his precious sense of honour, yet not really wanting him to. Emotionally she might fight against it, but it was all a part of what made him Chuck. Did she want him any other way?

Yes! screamed her body. She wanted him any way she could get him. No, her heart answered with its own sigh of regret. Irritation was raising its ugly head. Why, if he was going to suddenly cop out, did he raise her expectations at all?

Still she didn't move. His hands that for a while had been still had started to move again. Passion no longer drove them. They were heavy, moving slowly, and communicated their regret as they soothed the tingling skin on her shoulders, on her arms and her side.

'We would make a great pair, though,' he whispered. For the first time Barbara put the obvious meaning to the slur in his voice. Too much champagne too fast. She hadn't considered that, but in thinking about it she felt her irritation cool. She should have realised he was drinking it too fast, and probably on an empty stomach. She sighed, feeling cheated. She had thought he was finally beginning to recognise his feelings for her, and it was only light-headedness over alcohol.

For a while she just lay in his arms, crushed by her disappointment. When she realised his slow caresses had stopped, she rose up on one elbow and gazed at him. Forget light-headedness. He was drunk. And his even breathing warned her he was asleep. Her body was still outraged, but her mind had accepted the necessity. He lay so quiet, his face in sleep was smoothed of care.

The thought, a childlike innocence, crossed her mind but nothing about him was childlike. Where had she heard the words—the sleep of the deserving? The term fitted.

Reluctantly she disengaged herself and rose. Gently, so as not to wake him, she climbed over his still form and went into the bedroom to get a blanket and a pillow. As couches went, hers was comfortable, and he was in no condition to drive.

When she returned from the bedroom, he had moved away from the edge of the couch, and was in less danger of falling to the floor. She removed the cushions from the back to give him an extra few inches of space, slipped a pillow under his head and pulled off his shoes. As she tucked the blanket around him, she gave him a light kiss on the forehead. Yes, she thought. There was the nobility of knighthood in his face. Too bad he wore his armour for another lady.

'Good night, sweet lord—dream of fair deeds,' she murmured and turned off the lights.

The next morning, Barbara had the coffee perking and bacon in the microwave when Chuck woke up.

'Good morning,' she called as she heard him stirring.

'Oh, my head—oh, you wonderful person.'

The tearing of tinfoil and the plop-plop of the wafers in water told her he spotted the palliative and glass of water she had put on the coffee table.

'Can you take some breakfast?' she asked when she heard him stirring again.

'No, but I guess I'd better,' he replied. 'I've got to make a run today—lord, what time is it?'

'Just after five,' Barbara told him. Most of the drivers made earlier starts, but she had not thought he could handle it. 'You won't be disgracefully late. I put one of those disposable razors in the bathroom along with a new toothbrush.'

When he disappeared into the bathroom, she folded the blanket and put the cushions back on the sofa. All evidence of his night on the couch had been erased and she had set the table when he reappeared. That was some suit, she thought as he took the chair opposite hers. The fine material and good tailoring combined to make it look fresh even though he had slept in it.

He took tentative bites and sipped the coffee cautiously. For a few minutes he seemed to be concentrating on his breakfast, but Barbara knew what was on his mind. She had been steeling herself for his opening remarks since first opening her eyes that morning.

Not one to delay, he looked up, his face full of worry.

'I think I'd better do some apologising.'

'I think you should too,' Barbara laughed. 'What about my reputation? Passing out and sleeping on my sofa! My neighbours are going to gossip like crazy.'

'I'll try to get out of here before they're moving around, but that's not what I'm talking about.'

Barbara knew what was on his mind. She was prepared to lie her way through a brick wall if necessary, rather than have a discomfort grow between them. It certainly would if he remembered the night before, and apparently he did.

She looked up, her eyes narrowing. 'I don't care if you were too loaded to remember, you promised me that computer, and I expect it. Even if you did fall asleep while we were discussing which one.'

Chuck's brows drew together. 'We just said we'd get one—we didn't talk about brands—'

'We certainly did!' Barbara sounded convincing even to herself. 'I'm not surprised you don't remember it. I think you lived half a lifetime in dreams after I covered you with a blanket. You mumbled all night. But you promised me a computer—that was the last thing you said.'

Chuck kept staring at her, searching her face. 'That's all? Nothing else happened? We just discussed a computer? I seem to remember—'

Barbara interrupted him. 'If you remember promising me a mink coat, I'll take it, but I didn't want to push my luck too far.'

Chuck stared at his breakfast. 'I dreamed a lot, hunh?'

'You sounded as if you did—' She looked at him hopefully. 'Did you promise me something in your dreams that I'd like to have?'

'Uh—no—nothing about promises.' His relief left Barbara feeling a little sick. 'No dinner, that's what caused it,' he said. His voice was picking up life now that he was no longer worried. 'But I wish I hadn't killed the evening so fast. I sure didn't have much time to celebrate the new contract.

'Let's celebrate it again when you come back from this trip,' Barbara suggested. They had finished breakfast, and Chuck helped her clear the table. As they walked out to the car, he was in a thoughtful trance, but he looked up, his brows puckered.

'You make us a reservation at some fancy place for Thursday night—but make it where they speak English. And no baby chickens—I'll be hungry.'

CHAPTER NINE

EARLY Thursday afternoon, Barbara sat at her desk, stared at the shining surface and dreamed. Chuck was due back in town by four o'clock. Their reservations were confirmed at the Red Sails Inn. The famous sea-food restaurant was too crowded to be considered exclusive, but that was because people in all walks of life enjoyed the excellent food. Barbara had been licking her lips all week, thinking of their steak and lobster plate.

When the telephone rang she put out her hand as if trying to block off the noise. 'Oh, it's not him, he's on his way back with no trouble,' she said and would have made her words into a talisman of protection if she could.

But the caller wasn't Chuck.

'I would like to speak to Mr Ingram, if you please.' Barbara knew and dreaded that sultry voice. She held her breath, hoping inaction would keep away the pain. In desperation she fell back on the childish superstition, to hold the breath and wish helped make the wish come true. Maybe she had been mistaken in her recognition. Maybe it wasn't Sandy.

'May I please speak to Mr Ingram—that is if you're capable of telling him he has a call.'

No mistake. Sandy's cultured acid was unmistakable.

'I'm sorry, but he's out of town until later this afternoon,' Barbara answered. Again she longed to lie outrageously, to say he was gone for a month, anything to keep Chuck and Sandy from getting together,

161

but what would be the use? Spitefulness broughts its
own and often unwelcome payoffs. She promised to
have Chuck call when he came in, and hung up the
phone.

The afternoon dragged out her disappointment.
Hoping against hope, she delayed cancelling the reservation at the Red Sails Inn. Would they still go? He had
promised her they would. But would that promise hold
when he learned Sandy had returned from Europe
earlier than expected? No. He was a man of his word,
he'd just think Barbara wouldn't mind. She was not in a
position to tell him she would.

As she expected, he was elated to learn Sandy had
returned. All the fatigue of the hard trip fell away when
she gave him the message. Ignoring the rest of notes over
a four-day period he went into his office and closed the
door.

Barbara waited until she saw the light on the telephone that said his line was busy. She telephoned,
cancelling the reservation for dinner.

When he came back into her office and took his
customary chair across from her desk, part of his elation
had fallen away.

'Couldn't you reach her?' Barbara asked.

'Yeah, I got her,' he sounded flat, tired. 'She'd made
other plans for the evening.'

There must have been some censure in Barbara's
eyes, because he leaped to defend Sandy.

'She has friends everywhere, you know.'

'Of course,' Barbara tried to sound bright and
spritely. He must never know how much she disliked
Sandy or their relationship would suffer. What relationship? she wondered. If Sandy became Mrs Charles
Ingram, could Barbara even continue working for him,
loving him and knowing he belonged to another woman?

Her pride said no, but she could not imagine being anywhere else.

'Anyway, I was right to cancel the reservation for dinner,' Barbara added. 'You look tired. You need some rest.'

'Not before I tune up that Mercedes,' Chuck said quietly.

Naturally he wanted the car, now that Sandy was back. Barbara wondered how she let that detail slip her mind. But he looked so tired. He probably cheated on his log book, driving undeclared hours. He had been driving the GM diesel with the short wheelbase, and Barbara knew from short experience what that machine was like. He was bumped and jostled into exhaustion.

'Can't you put the car in the shop? I bet we could find some place that would take it tonight and have it ready tomorrow evening.' That was all she could offer as a suggestion.

'No, I've got to do it myself this first time. I need to know exactly what Gresham's great-nephew did to it. I wouldn't trust it, otherwise. Any chance Otis will be in today? I could sure use his help.'

Barbara didn't need to look at the driving schedule to know the answer. In Chuck's absence, she had sent Otis on an overnight run to Phoenix. He left that morning and was probably nearing his destination at that moment. She shook her head.

'Do you need someone else? Can I call someone?'

'No. I can do it alone. It's just faster if someone is around to fetch and carry.' He grinned. 'You know how big shots are. They always want someone to handle the little stuff.'

His sally had fallen a little short. He was too tired to be in top form.

'Have you had anything to eat?' Barbara asked. She

knew him well. He often skipped lunch on the road, trying to get in early. When he shook his head, she reached for her handbag. 'Let's go and feed your face. You'll have more energy to work on the car.'

But Chuck had a better idea. He would return some calls while she went for hamburgers. After he ate he could start tuning the Mercedes.

Halfway through his second hamburger he looked up. 'Are you sure you didn't want to go to the Red Sails Inn?'

'I'll skip it tonight, but at the first available opportunity I expect you to make up for that,' she told him, waving a chip for emphasis.

When he finished eating he stayed, talking for a few minutes, and Barbara felt for him as he walked back to his office to change into a pair of mechanic's overalls. His walk usually had the sensual grace of repressed strength and energy, but that afternoon he needed a force of will to keep him going. His shoulders were usually thrown back, more with the joy of living than arrogance, but now they were drooping. Not even knowing Sandy was in town had given him more than a momentary uplift.

While he changed clothes, Barbara carefully closed the cardboard boxes and put them back in the white bag from the fast food restaurant. She carried it out to the big dustbin at the rear of the yard. On the way back to the office, she passed Chuck, heading for the mechanics' shop.

Back in the office, Barbara watched him as he opened the bonnet on the car, managed to get the engine started, and stood listening to it. He needed a helper. As he said, someone to fetch and carry would cut down his working time.

'He's fixing that car so he can drive Sandy around,'

Barbara told herself. She spoke aloud, trying to make herself behave with some modicum of intelligence.

But he's so tired, her heart answered.

'No girl in her right mind would destroy her fingernails and get her hands stained with grease to help him impress another woman!'

But he's so tired.

'You're an idiot, a gold-medal idiot! You could win in the Olympics if they had an event in stupidity!' she chastised herself as she headed for Chuck's office and the cupboard where he kept the commercial laundry. She remembered the delivery of several pairs of overalls in the weekly delivery.

'What is this?' Chuck looked up as she leaned over the open bonnet of the Mercedes. She forgave him for the chuckle that escaped before he stopped it. She had pulled her hair up on her head and covered it with an old baseball cap he used when he crawled under the trucks. The overall was too large for her, so she had turned back both the cuffs and the trousers. Below the rolled trouser legs her feet looked incongruous in red, high-heeled sandals.

'One mechanic's helper, reporting for duty,' she announced, saluting. At his doubtful look, she raised her chin, trying to look haughty. 'I do know a grease-gun from a Crescent.' She did. The grease-gun had a flexible tube on the end, and a handle that pumped. She decided not to tell him she and the Crescent wrench had never met. Her entire mechanical ability was exhausted in using a tin opener.

Chuck grinned and shook his head. Still she could tell by his lightening attitude that he was glad she was there.

'Why don't you make us a pot of coffee? Then if you really want to help you can sit and listen to me swear.'

'There's the coffee,' Barbara pointed to the large red,

rolling tool-box where two steaming cups rested among
the wrenches. 'And I came to hand you things—to fetch
and carry.'

'Okay—' Chuck sounded doubtful, but apparently
she was accepted. Since he had stopped to talk to her, he
took the coffee and sipped at it while he stared into the
engine. Barbara walked over and cocked her head to
one side and stared down at the conglomeration of wires
and parts and engine and stuff that made no sense to her
at all.

'Doesn't look too bad,' she said judiciously. 'Possibly
needs a new fan-belt. Do we need to flush the radiator?'
She had heard mechanics in service stations make those
suggestions.

Chuck bit his lips and tried to keep away his smile. 'I
don't think so, but maybe we could adjust the tyres and
rotate the spark plugs.' That sounded strange to
Barbara, and she could tell by his dancing eyes he was
making some joke. She raised her chin and looked
haughty again, not daring an answer in her ignorance.
She knew tyres were rotated, but spark plugs? Better to
keep her mouth shut.

'What's this?' Barbara eyed a bucket of liquid that
smelled suspiciously like petrol, but the dark colour told
her it was not meant to be put in her petrol tank.

'It's solvent. I use it to clean parts—and tools.' His
reply was muffled as he leaned over the engine. Barbara
nodded after listening to make sure he was not teasing
her again. She strolled over to see if she could be of
assistance, but he had cloths spread over the bumper,
and by him were several wrenches and some odd looking
things. To her it seemed he had enough for the moment,
and she had discovered how to be of help.

Inside the shop she found a small brush and a stack of
commercial paper towels, the strong fibrous type used

for cleaning windscreens. While she was waiting, she would make herself useful cleaning the tools. They would fit the bolts and nuts better if they were clean, she reasoned.

She started with something she knew about. The polished chrome cylinder with a square hole at one end was a ratchet, she knew. She dumped two boxes on the asphalt and wiped out the boxes with a towel dampened in solvent. Then systematically she cleaned the sockets, deciding while she was at it to improve Chuck's method of storing them. Sheer inefficiency to have one of each size in each box. She put all the small ones together and all the large ones in the other box

She was finished and putting the n back in the drawers of the red tool box when Chuck turned around.

'What are you doing?'

'I'm straightening out these sockets—you had them all messed up,' she said as she cleaned her hands. 'I put all ones for the cars together, and the ones for the trucks together. Now when you service a truck you just pull out the box with the big ones—and those that fit the cars will be out of the way.'

Chuck's silence was solid enough to stop an eighteen-wheeler. Finally he managed to choke out two words.

'You didn't.' His voice, slightly incredulous, broke on the second word.

'When you get used to it, you'll like it,' Barbara spoke with the confidence of a business-school graduate who took a course in filing. 'There are so *many* of them— I bet you spend half your time looking for what you want.'

'Not like I'm going to,' he answered weakly. He leaned against the car, all his strength seemed to be gone. 'Babs—have you ever heard of metric and American standard?'

'Of course. We're switching, but what has that got to do with a good system for storing your tools?'

Chuck shook his head. He seemed to be having trouble getting his thoughts together. 'We're switching. Vehicles are not adjustable. Some have American standard fittings, others—Sadie and the Mercedes have Metric.'

Barbara's pride in her work took a quick dive. 'I goofed?'

'Oh no. Not until you start putting them in manila file folders.' With the speed of carefully controlled patience, Chuck spread several paper towels on the ground, took the two boxes and sat down on the concrete. 'I'll have to sort them out now, or I'll be searching all night,' he said.

Barbara knelt by him. Better, she thought, if she could have crawled under the asphalt. Her intention was to help him. Instead she had added to his work. And she appreciated his patience, even though she knew he was holding the lid on it by sheer force.

'Could I help if you showed me the difference?' she asked meekly. 'Is it something you have to know by experience, or—'

Chuck's glance was not the friendliest, but he relented. 'No. See this one, with 5/8" engraved on it?'

'I see it.'

'The ones with fractions are American standard. You find those. Put them in that box. There are several different sets.'

Relieved she could at least help straighten out the mess, she worked quietly for a few minutes. Chuck's '*Now* what are you doing?' sounded desperate.

Barbara pointed to each of the neat rows in turn. 'These are quarters—these are eighths—sixteenths and thirty-seconds. You said there were several sets.'

Chuck's silent stare told her she was wrong again. 'That's not what you meant either?'

'Damn, am I glad you're not a book-keeper. You'd probably total them into one gigantic socket!' His patience was at an end. He looked around and Barbara could feel his desire for something on which to vent his anger. 'I can just see that monster,' he yelled. 'It'll sneak out at night, and howl at the street lights. It'll bite cars and suck their oil!' After letting off steam on his mythical creature he sat shaking his head.

Barbara couldn't blame him. And what had been wrong with her thinking? She knew five-sixteenths came after one quarter, and the thirty-seconds fitted in somewhere in between. She'd have to do some mental arithmetic to figure out which was where. Her mind had been so full of her original goof, she made another, more foolish than the first. Wonder if there was anything higher than a gold medal for being an idiot? The congressional medal of stupid?

'Even I know better than that,' she said softly and started making one row where she had four.

Chuck's arm fell around her shoulders. Once he had vented his frustrations, he was back to his usual warm, understanding self. 'Stop looking like a five-year-old who failed kindergarten,' he said. 'Maybe we should go back to your other idea. It could be easier. Cars and trucks—' he broke off to laugh. 'But you know, you didn't take into account the whole series of vehicles. We could split them up for motorcycles, small cars, large cars, step-vans—'

'You forgot bicycles,' Barbara objected as she joined the play. If he was willing to put aside his anger over the extra work she'd caused, she was going to do her part to make the situation easier.

'Oh, tricycles too.' Chuck grinned as he put one tiny

rachet on its side and by flicking a finger, sent it rolling in her direction.

'Here's one for a step-van,' Barbara imitated his method of transferring the cylinder from her group to his.

'Take that, that and that for the big rigs,' Chuck rolled three large pieces across. The third came with enough force to skitter into several smaller ones and send them sailing.

'You just shot all my little ones for rollerskates,' Barbara complained and scrambled to catch the rolling rachets before they went under the Mercedes.

'Children at play?'

The new voice belonged to Sandy. Barbara, stretched out, almost falling on her side as she reached under the car for one of the sockets, was frozen by the iciness in the question. She had heard that voice on the phone often enough to recognise it. Could she crawl under the car and simply refuse to face her rival? But cowards died how many deaths? Her glance went first to Chuck who, like her, had been caught in the ice. He sat hunched over the tools he was sorting, his head raised, his mouth at half-cock by the unexpectedness of Sandy's arrival. Never one to hesitate long, Chuck uncrossed his legs and stood.

Barbara turned to get a good look at her rival. Her first impression seemed to stop her breathing. Sultry Sandy had been the right name after all. Barbara could not remember ever seeing a more beautiful woman, though she hadn't expected her to be so petite. She could not have been more than five feet two, and the silver trouser suit left no doubt she was perfectly pro-portioned. Her long black hair was pulled to the side and fell across her shoulder with an allure many women tried for and seldom achieved. Her startling blue-violet eyes passed over Barbara with a dismissal too instantaneous to have held any appraisal. The ultimate insult of one woman for another.

While Barbara remained on the ground, Chuck followed Sandy as she walked back across the yard to her car. Their conversation was too low voiced for Barbara to hear, and she made no effort to listen. She was still shocked by her first sight of her rival. She was competing against that? No way, she told herself. No wonder Chuck was knocked sideways every time Sandy came back to town. What man wouldn't be? She looked at her hands, dirty from working with the sockets, and she had broken a nail. But what did it matter? Chuck would never notice. Not with that beauty back in town.

With a heart like lead, she continued to sort out the mess she had made, refusing even to look up. The last thing she wanted to see was Chuck and Sandy together.

After a few minutes the sports car roared off and she heard Chuck's slow footsteps coming across the asphalt yard. Barbara still kept her eyes down. By his walk, he had suffered from the encounter, she decided. He wouldn't want her or anyone else to see his downcast look.

He stopped just in front of her. 'Think you can finish that?' He sounded tired, beaten down.

'I think so,' Barbara was almost whispering to keep her own emotions out of her voice. 'Make complete sets—one of every size in metric and—'

'And American standard, that's a good girl. I'll see if I can straighten out the car's problems.'

She was just finishing when the sputtering in the idling engine smoothed out to a silken purr. When he accelerated the growl of power was full-throated and even.

'I wonder why I didn't try that first. It was obvious all the time,' he muttered.

Barbara slid the metal boxes back in the drawers and looked over at him. 'Remember looking for trees in the forest?' She was wasting her time with hints and innuendos, she decided. She wasn't going to reach him. Now that she'd seen Sandy, she knew that.

Chuck nodded absently and put away his equipment. He rolled the big tool box back into the shop, closing and locking the door.

'I'm hungry again,' he said. 'Let's go and get some scrambled eggs at Johnnie's.'

'You don't like that place,' Barbara warned him. Neither of them cared for the little greasy cafe two blocks from the office.

'I'm too tired to change clothes again, so let's settle for it anyway.'

Barbara followed him as he headed for the office and noticed the set of his shoulders. They carried a defensiveness that overrode his fatigue. With his every step, her own lightened. By refusing to change out of his overalls, he was making an unconscious but definitive statement. She had seen him so exhausted he was grey in the face, but he was never sloppy or allowed the grime of his work to remain unnecessarily. He was not fastidious, but he took a certain pride in his appearance.

Unconsciously he was fighting something Sandy had said. Barbara had no idea what it might be, but Chuck was reacting by being seen in his mechanic's outfit. Without realising it, he was defending himself and what he was.

Suddenly the darkening evening seemed lighter. Sandy might be one of the world's beauties, but she certainly didn't know how to handle her man. And she'd given Barbara a strong weapon.

'Let me wash my face and hands. Then you can dress,' Chuck said as they entered the office.

'I don't think I'll dress either,' Barbara answered.

'*You're* not going out like that?' Chuck grinned. To Barbara, that silly smile was like sunshine.

'Why not?' she asked as she pulled off her cap and shook out her hair. 'Mechanicking is honest work. What should I be ashamed of?' She marched by him, heading for the bathroom. She couldn't fight Sandy in looks. The socialite's outfit had shown her all her spent money and effort would never put her in the same class. All she had to offer was her honest approval of Chuck and her unqualified support. She was going to make the most of it and hope it was enough.

By the time they finished the scrambled eggs and bacon, Chuck was relaxing, the tension brought on by Sandy's visit had disappeared. He was on his second cup of coffee when the smooth skin around the edges of his eyes started crinkling. He was having some trouble holding his mouth straight.

'What are you thinking? Something I wouldn't like,' Barbara accused.

'I can't get over you—filing my sockets by size—the little ones for the cars—'

'That's enough of that!' Barbara hefted a salt shaker, as if to throw it at him. 'You didn't have to make those cracks, and what about shooting them like marbles? You started that.'

'Yeah,' Chuck laughed. But his happy memories seemed to fade. He looked slightly ashamed as if he had been caught in some mildly improper act. His mouth tightened, impatience seemed to be taking the place of his embarrassment. 'People shouldn't waste their time on kids' games.'

Kids' games—children at play. He was paraphrasing Sandy's remark. Barbara suddenly felt so frustrated she wanted to hit something. Couldn't he see what that female was doing to him. She wouldn't stop until she took all the fun out of his life. Didn't he see she kept her nose in the air and wanted him to live by her standards? No, he wouldn't see that. Love provided its own blinders, and in Chuck's case they were three feet thick. But Sandy had not succeeded in turning him into a bored sophisticate yet. He started grinning again.

'I surprised myself, hitting those little ones like I did. I'm pretty good at that.'

'I might have done better if *I* had tried a larger size,' Barbara countered. 'Tomorrow I'll take you on again and we'll see.'

The reversal had been only temporary. Chuck's face closed again. 'We'll see,' he answered. Non-committal. An answer for a child. He was playing grown-up again to please Sandy.

Barbara made no answer. She would have to wait; to continue the game when he was attempting to disparage it would ruin it for both of them. They finished their coffee and he walked her to her car. She was inside when he leaned over and flicked at a strand of her hair.

'You know, you make a pretty good beginner. The next time we work on a car, bring a piece of chalk.'

Barbara was puzzled. 'Chalk?'

'So we can draw a ring. If we're going to use sockets as marbles, we'll have to have a regular game.'

'I get to choose my aggie,' Barbara retorted, starting the car. As she drove to her flat, she wondered how long he'd hold his mood before Sandy's attitude intruded again. Would he keep swinging back and forth like a pendulum, or take a position? He would make up his mind, she decided. And when he did, his decision would affect the rest of her life.

CHAPTER TEN

THE next morning, Barbara started the office coffee-pot, put the mechanic's overalls in the laundry bag and was at her desk when Chuck came in. By his expression he wanted to tease her about the night before, but the ringing telephone stopped him.

The newest truck in the fleet had eaten its fan belt, and was stalled on Route 5, halfway between San Diego and Los Angeles. The driver didn't have a spare.

'Do me a favour and call the club. Make reservations for me,' Chuck said as he grabbed the keys to the jeep.

Barbara sorted the mail and jabbed at the phone as she dialled the club. Each time she pushed the dial around, she felt as if she were adding another nail to the coffin of her hopes. And why did she have to do it? Making a reservation for him to take out another woman was more than she should have to bear.

She finished the call and sat staring through the window, succumbing to the morose, when the phone rang again. Wondering if she too might have to deliver a fan belt, she picked up the receiver. If Jim Dennis was having mechanical problems he didn't say. He did ask her to have dinner with him. Some friends were having an anniversary party.

Well, why not? It would be better than sitting at home, wallowing in self-pity. She agreed, gave him her address so he could pick her up at eight, and when the call was finished, tried to get some work done. Her mind kept straying back to the night before, thinking of Chuck's swings of mood as he tried to accept Sandy's way of thinking, yet his basic nature fought it.

She wished he would make up his mind. Every time he swung, she was pulled off course. If he had made up his mind about Sandy, she wished he would settle it. One blow, one final blow would be better than the hope and hurt rollercoaster she was riding.

She pulled her mind back to the job, yanked two letters from the drawer—she had filed them under 'B' for bills of lading, rather than by company.

When Chuck returned from his trip up the freeway, he spent the rest of the afternoon doing a safety check on the vehicle he had driven to Denver.

Barbara finished her work, and not wanting to infect him with her glum mood, she took the rest of the afternoon off. At home she did her laundry, cleaned the flat and took a leisurely bath. She spent hours getting ready for her date with Jim. The pale cream-coloured silk suit with blue trim suited her complexion, showed off her figure and did all the things it was supposed to, but she couldn't take any pleasure in wearing it. She bought it to impress Chuck. He wouldn't see it. Even if he did, the memory of Sandy's chic clothes would put her in the shade.

'Is this okay?' she asked the picture on the front of *Mediterranean Magic*.

Melissa and Damon seemed far away, as if they'd given up on Barbara and no longer took an interest in her affairs.

'I don't blame you,' she sympathised. Her life was such a muddle even she wanted to forget all about it.

Used to Chuck arriving half an hour early, she was half irritated with Jim who arrived five minutes late.

'Uhm-m,' he murmured when she opened the door. 'Good evening, beautiful lady.' His reaction to her appearance was perfect. If Chuck had said those words they would have thrilled her. She tried to smile at Jim.

Now why couldn't I develop an interest in someone like him, she asked herself as they walked out to the car. He might be a wolf, but that was possibly because he was really searching for someone. At least his heart wasn't spoken for. His tall, well-built frame complemented his clothing and he was strikingly handsome. His eyes danced with laughter, and he had a ready wit. And he wasn't Chuck.

His Ferrari eased out of the parking space in front of the building with the controlled energy of a land-bound jet. To Barbara it seemed to strain against his light foot on the accelerator as if it wanted to turn the city street into a race-course.

'By the way, I'm bringing you out on false pretences,' Jim said.

'Oh?'

'There really was an anniversary party planned. But when the hostess breaks her leg, what do you do?'

'I'm so sorry.' Barbara wondered if she sounded sufficiently regretful. She could feel for the hostess, but she was more concerned about what happened now. She had nothing in common with Jim Dennis, and spending an evening alone with him could be a strain.

'I thought we might join Marie and Frank if that's okay with you.'

Barbara readily agreed. She was genuinely fond of Marie Dennis. At least they had one thing in common. They both disliked Sandy Harrington.

But when Jim turned on to a street that was becoming increasingly familiar, and swung the Ferrari between the stone columns of the country club drive, Barbara was ready to sink. She should have expected it, perhaps, but it had not occurred to her that they would be going to the club. That was the last place she wanted to be.

Chuck and Sandy would be there or arriving soon.
Only the night before she had decided she could not
compete with Sandy on her own ground. How was she to
get out of entering that door, she wondered. Short of
feigning a broken leg herself, she couldn't see a way.
While an attendant drove the car away, Jim led her into
the cocktail lounge. Barbara's heart felt as if some
disaster waited just past those doors.

'Barbara! This is a wonderful surprise!' Marie's voice
came out of a dim corner, but her joy seemed real and
Barbara felt better just hearing her. The room was
crowded, and Jim moved ahead, acting the part of a
trail-blazer among the waiters and milling patrons of the
club. They found Marie and her husband Frank nursing
glasses of white wine and trying to peer over the heads of
the mob.

'You've saved our evening,' Marie said as she moved
her chair slightly so Jim and Barbara could move their
seats out of the well travelled aisle between the massive
Spanish-style tables and the dark, carved chairs. 'The
fiesta has really brought in a crowd, and our guests had
some emergency.'

'Not another broken leg?' Barbara asked. She felt
ashamed of herself, but two emergencies in one night?

'Broken leg?' Marie looked blank. Jim explained to
Marie. Barbara was glad no one at the table took her
remark in bad part. The blank look on Marie's face and
the detailed story Jim told seemed genuine.

'Joyce?' Marie sounded shocked. 'Frank, darling, you
remember Joyce and Carl—we met them at the
Reynolds' party—' While Marie related a short story to
help Frank remember the unfortunate Joyce, Barbara
gave herself a mental dressing-down. She was letting her
own disappointment and her wariness of Jim make her
oversuspicious. If she behaved badly she would only be

spoiling the evening for all of them.

She was letting Jim's reputation colour her opinion. Certainly she had no fault to find with Marie and Frank. The vivacious, dark-haired woman obviously adored her husband, though he was not exactly hero material in the sense of the modern romantic novels. A small, spare man, he looked years older than Jim. He was going bald, a slight paunch and lack of tan indicated he seldom joined the others on the tennis courts.

When a waiter appeared, telling them their table was ready, they trooped into the dining-room where decorations had transformed the room and the raised dais was covered by a palm-frond roofed framework. Beneath it, instruments were set up in readiness for a band.

Probably some Mexican fiesta being used as an excuse for a turnout, Barbara surmised. She had no idea which one. When she first arrived in San Diego, she had seen banners over the doors of some stores and kept waiting for the big fiesta. A year later she discovered *Habla Español* was not a holiday.

Dinner that night was buffet-style. The food was entirely Mexican, but many of the dishes were new to her, and she enjoyed experimenting.

Barbara thought she would have enjoyed the evening more if her eyes had not strayed to the door so often. Jim and Frank, wrangling good-naturedly over some happening at the office, had not noticed. Marie had, she knew. The dark beauty's sparkling eyes told her she knew what Barbara expected, and tried to keep her entertained.

'— and so when their sister started in labour, naturally they gave us the brush-off. I warn you, don't *ever* plan an evening with two sisters if their younger one is expecting a baby,' Marie was saying as she indicated the two empty places at the table. 'And by the time they remembered to call me, we were just leaving for the club. Twin boys. Three days from now, and they'll be taking over the babies and their younger sister will—'

Marie babbled on, but Barbara ceased to hear a word. Chuck and Sandy stood in the doorway. The head waiter was making some explanation that required a good deal of hand-waving. Jim, looking up, followed the direction of Barbara's gaze.

'Isn't that Chuck?' he asked.

'Apparently they can't get a table,' Frank said. 'There was some mix-up tonight—two reservation lists or something. They made more promises than they can keep. If you know them, we have some empty places.' He winked at Marie. 'Then you'll have your happy party again.'

'That remains to be seen,' Marie said *sotto voce* to Barbara. 'Frank doesn't know Sandy.'

The two women exchanged understanding looks and Barbara tried to look pleased. Her disaster had arrived in a little white frock that whispered of Parisian show-rooms and what Sandy did for it paled the original model to nothing. Barbara had caught her breath over the price of the silk suit she wore, but compared to Sandy's outfit, she could have bought it in the dime store.

Jim hurried to the door and led the couple back to the table.

'Insufferable,' Sandy was saying. 'There will be complaints to the management tomorrow.' She didn't have to add she would be one of the ones making trouble. That sparkled out of her blue-violet eyes.

Chuck looked as if he had just been offered a reprieve. He was not the type to take the incident as a personal insult, but she knew he wanted the evening to go off well. Was she mistaken, or did his eyes light up when he realised she was at the table? They darkened again when he made the connection between Jim Dennis and herself, but Marie was demanding his attention once the introductions were over.

'I saw one of your trucks the other day.' She made it sound as if it were a great adventure for which she should have been rewarded. 'Don't you have an arrow under the name?'

'That's us,' Chuck grinned and gave a half nod at Barbara, including her in the credit. 'Where was it?'

'Going east on Route 8, if I remember right.'

'Then I was probably driving it,' Chuck said. 'I need some good men—anyone want a job?' That brought a laugh from everyone but Sandy. She was staring at Barbara.

'Men? Is that discrimination?' Marie demanded. Another laugh around the table.

'Good things happening?' Jim asked.

'The future has that rosy tinge at the moment.' Chuck gave a slight smile. His qualification at the end was a graceful attempt to cover any boastfulness. Refusing to brag, he gave the impression of constant success that was too commonplace to be much noticed. Barbara saw Frank's interest in this new arrival grow.

Suddenly Marie turned on Barbara. 'I still think that was discrimination. Does he ever let you drive a truck?'

'If he *lets* me drive a truck, I'll look for another job,' Barbara retorted. 'Getting behind the steering wheel of one of those monsters would scare me to death.'

'I'd think you'd feel like a king,' Marie sounded a little wistful. Here was clearly a woman who loved new experiences.

During this exchange, Sandy had been watching Barbara. With perfectly manicured nails, she roughened the iron-polished smoothness of the linen napkin that was part of her table setting.

'Yes, I believe you prefer to be under the vehicles, don't you?'

A short silence rolled around the table with all the mental decibels of a thunderclap. Chuck looked shocked.

His eyes sent Barbara a message—she didn't mean it the way it sounded.

Of course not, Barbara returned. She hoped he read it correctly; it was hard to lie with the eyes.

'You're a mechanic too?' Frank asked, leaning over, giving Barbara a smile. He was a fast man on the uptake. Obviously he'd caught the stab and was offering the salve of interest.

'Oh, she's a great one,' Chuck answered for her and started telling about her fiasco in sorting the sockets. He was speaking a little too fast, a little breathlessly as he tried to smooth over Sandy's insult. Jim, Frank and Marie were listening with a false intensity. Barbara was grateful for their support. Across the table, Sandy's deep-blue eyes were snapping with irritation. Apparently she had not expected a phalanx of support for Barbara.

While the men laughed at the story, Marie assumed a false brightness. 'I'm still not persuaded Barbara wasn't right,' she announced. She turned to offer her opinion directly. 'You were perfectly right, but their male egos won't admit it.'

Her remark brought Marie under the fire of the male teasing, suddenly interrupted by Sandy.

'Why don't I remember seeing you the night of the Wilsons' *bon voyage* party? Were you here? You weren't at the Christmas or the New Year's dances either, were you?'

The interruption was enough to bring silence, but something unknown to either Barbara or Chuck was happening. Both the Dennis men were parting their lips and filling their lungs to answer. Marie took the initiative away from them. Her face said this was woman's work.

'We weren't members at that time.' The unspoken question was answered. Barbara's and Chuck's confusion settled.

'Then you've only been members for a short time?' Translation: Johnny-come-latelys with no better taste than to accept one of Barbara's sort into their midst. Inference: Who are you to support someone *I* choose not to accept?

'Members only for a short time,' Marie agreed. Her eyes held Sandy's. If they had been eight-year-old boys, one would have been drawing a line, daring the other to cross.

Chuck's eyes were talking to Barbara again—Sandy's tired, it's just jet-lag, maybe she doesn't feel well—she's been doing too much. He was manufacturing reasons, trying to find excuses for what he could neither ignore or condone. Along with his excuses came his pain, his confusion.

Barbara accepted every excuse he offered, though they grew vague and half-formed, as he searched for any thread of thought that could bind his crumbling idealism of Sandy back to its untained glory.

'I want to dance,' Jim said abruptly. Not 'May I have the honour,' or even 'Let's dance.' He was fleeing the battle-zone with too much haste to worry about courtesy. Barbara was just glad he remembered to take her with him.

They edged into the crowd of moving bodies and swayed to the music, keeping the beat rather than attempting to make a show of the intricate Latin steps of the tango.

'What a bitch!' Jim muttered just loud enough for Barbara to hear.

'A very beautiful one,' Barbara reminded him. She was wondering if that beauty could hold Chuck.

'So is a python. Now I know what Marie meant when she said I should cross Sandy's trail—' he looked startled at his own words. In spite of her misery, Barbara ducked her head and smiled. She could imagine the rest of what Marie had said. Jim was a troller. He was always out to snare a new female, and Marie probably suggested Sandy would be a quick cure for his wandering. Sandy had shocked him into letting the society-stud image slip a bit. That gave her a new insight to the Dennises. Like Chuck, they were people working their way up in the world, and the snobbery of Sandy's ilk had yet to form, if it ever would.

But that didn't solve her problem. She could not go back to that table. She was the catalyst that brought on Sandy's rudeness. Maybe Chuck was right when he gave her excuses. Jet-lag, or an oncoming illness, had been the reason, and Barbara was just the last straw.

Remembering his hurt and confusion, she knew Sandy had shown him a new side of herself that night. Maybe she was usually a nicer person. Marie had indicated she was not. But if Marie disliked her for another reason, her opinion could be distorted. Marie? She seemed to like everyone but Sandy.

Barbara's thoughts were tumbling over each other as she tried to bring the evening into perspective. At the moment, only one thing was clear. She did not want to go back to that table. If she left, she would take with her most of the reason for Sandy's bad temper. To stay would only cause a scene that would hurt Chuck. It might open his eyes, but the pain it would bring was more than she could inflict on him. She looked up at Jim.

'Will you take me home?'

'I'll take you anywhere to get out of here. Does it have to be home?'

'This evening started out too badly to end well,' Barbara said with a sigh.

He was too intelligent to argue with her. 'Then let's go now, while they're dancing, and away from the table.'

On the way to her flat, Jim tried to call back the charm that kept many women interested, but between the scene at the club, and Barbara's lack of response, he gave it up. He didn't try to persuade her when she told him she would rather he did not come in with her.

After the door to her flat was closed, Barbara let her shoulders slump, their droop nearly as low as her spirits. Tonight had answered one question for her. If Chuck married Sandy, she would have to find another job. He would be out of her life completely. Even the innocent pleasure of working with him would be taken from her.

She doubted if she would have been able to stay anyway. But what would she do?

She thought back on her year and a half in San Diego, and realised that except for knowing how to get about, she was still virtually a stranger. At first learning her job and decorating her flat had taken all her time. Later Chuck had become the most important—no, he had become her life. She spoke to her neighbours, but she had never tried to be friends. That would have taken time from Chuck.

In one stroke she would be losing both him and her job, and her life consisted of nothing else. What was the question—does a gun no one hears make a noise? When Chuck wasn't there, would Barbara even exist? Not the part of her she had come to know the best—of that she was sure.

Unable to face the misery any more, she walked to her

favourite chair and sat, her handbag still in her hand. Her mind blanked itself out, letting the unworded sorrow have full sway. She was aware of the passing of time, but had no idea how long she sat there when she was pulled back into her miserable world by a knock on the door. She couldn't answer. She couldn't face anyone.

The knocking became a pounding. If she didn't answer, the entire building would be up in arms. She stood up, walking with a limp because she had kicked off one shoe and had forgotten about it. Entering the hall, she threw the locks without asking who her visitor was. The danger of not inquiring first occured to her, but what did it matter if someone knocked her on the head.

When she opened the door, Chuck strode in. His tie was loose, his jacket was open and his hands were in his pockets. The sideways tilt of his head told her he was pleased about something. Barbara wondered dully if he had come to tell her he was marrying Sandy. His first words could have meant just that.

'I made the grade,' he said. 'I'm a hero.'

'Of course you are—you always were,' Barbara answered, wondering when he was going to drop the bomb and end her world.

He leaned against the wall and stared out into space. 'Yep. I'm a full-fledged romantic hero that could be in any book. I've got the main talent for it.'

'Something special,' Barbara said. By agreeing, she was getting the opportunity to admit to all the things she had wanted to tell him. But what was he really saying?

'Yeah, that special something that keeps him from knowing the Melissas from the Zeldas until the end of the book.'

What? What *was* he saying? Shivers started up her back, ran down her arms and legs, but she refused to allow herself hope.

'Sandy?' Barbara could barely get out the word, but she had to know.

He was staring off into space again. 'Sandy was just a name.'

'She's also a beautiful woman,' Barbara reminded him. She wasn't going to let him build her hopes and dash them again.

'Not *my* Sandy—nor my heroine. You know, we never had that much time together. I've been driving around thinking about it. You see, I had a memory of a physical woman, but most of her, her generous nature, her sense of humour, her genuine concern for people —all that I made up in my mind, and I made up excuses when she didn't show those talents—but that's not quite right.' He stopped staring off into space; he looked Barbara straight in the eye. He reached out a raised a handful of her hair, letting the strands slip through his fingers in a golden shower. 'She was patterned after someone, I was just colour-blind on hair. My heroine would have left the club tonight rather than embarrass everyone with a scene.'

Barbara stayed still. Not by a muscle or a thought would she move. He had to say more. He did. He stuffed his hands back in his pockets and stared at the ceiling again. His stance was all bravado, as if he were standing up to some battle he wasn't sure of winning.

'Now, according to the books we read, the heroine is supposed to forgive the hero for his blindness and admit she loved him from the first. Otherwise he should pick her up, throw her on his trusty steed and gallop away into the night.' He gave her a pitiful look. 'Will you do your part? The Mercedes broke down again.'

She admitted to nothing. She just stepped into his arms and accepted his kiss, knowing this one was hers and she would never again wonder if his thoughts would be on another woman when he held her. Time passed unnoticed as she clung to him and when the kiss was over she laid her head on his shoulder.

'I thought you were going to marry her,' Barbara finally said.

'That makes two fools. Maybe it taught us something.' He held her. They were still as he seemed to be thinking. When he spoke he was thoughtful. 'I think we'll keep the membership at the club. Sandy can go to hell.' He looked slightly embarrassed at his bluntness. He was still his old chivalrous self. Then he forgot it and continued, 'People like the Dennises make it worthwhile.' He raised her chin. His face was serious. 'One day we'll have some glamour in our lives. We'll go to all those great places. People can envy us. Right now all I can offer is a lot of work, a few laughs, and some great dreams.'

'Is there anything better?' Barbara asked. Her emotions threatened to give way.

'Not when they're shared.' He held her close for a moment and then moved her to arms' length. 'But I'm not all that interested in glamour right now. I walked twenty blocks. Can I have a beer?'

Barbara laughed and turned towards the kitchen, but he held her back. 'Go and find your shoe and let me get it. Want one?'

'Sure,' she said. No champagne would ever taste better than that particular beer, she thought.

When he started for the kitchen, she removed her other shoe, walked over to the coffee-table and pushed the flowered centrepiece to one side. She picked up a small cushion and carefully placed it beside the first where he propped his feet. As she sat back and tried out the second small pillow she heard the tinkle of glasses and the pop-hiss of the opening beer cans. The sound reminded her of their conversation at dinner the night Sandy came back into their lives.

'Hey, hero!' she called out.

'Yeah?'

'When you pour that beer, easy on the heads!'

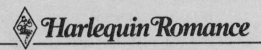
Harlequin Romance

Coming Next Month

2839   ODD MAN OUT   Sharron Cohen
A chauffeur's daughter's hand in marriage is priceless—both to
her fiancé and to his estranged brother, her first great love.
Would he use that love just to give his rival a run for his money?

2840   FOR KARIN'S SAKE   Samantha Day
A young widow is just beginning to feel whole again when
her heart goes out to a troubled child and her uncompromising
father. But is he suggesting marriage—just for the sake of
his daughter?

2841   THE MARATI LEGACY   Dana James
Although she's still haunted by the pain of a past experience, an
oceanographer joins a search for sunken treasure off the
Madagascar coast. She finds adventure, but she also finds
love—and is frightened by its intensity.

2842   IMMUNE TO LOVE   Claudia Jameson
No one is immune to love. But when a career girl falls for her
charming boss, she's afraid she'll contract permanent
heartache. Unless she can discover why he suddenly pulls away
from her...

2843   RING OF CLADDAGH   Annabel Murray
Claddagh Hall is left jointly to a London fashion designer and
the rightful heir, a provocative and teasing Irishman. But it's no
joking matter when he proposes marriage!

2844   MOROCCAN MADNESS   Angela Wells
After their whirlwind courtship, her Moroccan husband
accused her of betraying him on their wedding night. Now he
wants her back. To continue the madness that drove her away?
Or to rekindle the love that still smolders between them?

Available in June wherever paperback books are sold, or
through Harlequin Reader Service.

In the U.S.
901 Fuhrmann Blvd.
P.O. Box 1397
Buffalo, N.Y. 14240-1397

In Canada
P.O. Box 603
Fort Erie, Ontario
L2A 5X3